Funny stories for 5 year olds

Helen Paiba was one of the most committed, knowledgeable and acclaimed children's booksellers in Britain. For more than twenty years she owned and ran the Children's Bookshop in Muswell Hill, London, which under her guidance gained a superb reputation for its range of children's books and for the advice available to its customers.

Helen was also involved with the Booksellers Association for many years and served on both its Children's Bookselling Group and the Trade Practices Committee.

In 1995 she was given honorary life membership of the Booksellers Association of Great Britain and Ireland in recognition of her outstanding services to the association and to the book trade. In the same year the Children's Book Circle (sponsored by Books for Children) honoured her with the Eleanor Farjeon Award, given for distinguished service to the world of children's books.

Books in this series

Funny Stories for 5 Year Olds

Funny Stories for 6 Year Olds

Funny Stories for 7 Year Olds

Funny Stories for 8 Year Olds

Funny stories

for **5** year olds

Chosen by Helen Paiba

Illustrated by Christyan Fox

MACMILLAN CHILDREN'S BOOKS

First published 2000 by Macmillan Children's Books

This edition published 2016 by Macmillan Children's Books
an imprint of Pan Macmillan
20 New Wharf Road, London N1 9RR
Associated companies throughout the world
www.panmacmillan.com

ISBN 978-1-5098-0493-1

Typeset by SX Composing DTP, Rayleigh, Essex
Printed and bound by CPI Group (UK) Ltd, Croydon CR0 4YY

Contents

Three Cheers for Charlie!

Pat Hutchins

Once there was a fat pink pig called Charlie, who lived on a little farm in the middle of the country. Charlie had a cousin, who was a fat pink pig called James, who lived in a little house in the middle of the town.

One day, Charlie said, "My cousin James is coming to stay," and all the animals were very excited.

"I wonder if he looks like Our

1

Charlie," they asked each other.

Well, if they'd seen Charlie and James taking their baths, they would have thought they were as alike as two peas in a pod.

But when they saw them dressed, they soon spotted the difference.

"My word, Our Charlie," they all said when they met James. "What a splendid fellow your cousin is. Just look at that hat!"

And they all admired the black, shiny top hat that perched nicely on the top of James's head.

And then they looked at the patched cloth cap that kept slipping over Charlie's eyes.

"And just look at those clothes, Our Charlie," they said, admiring the long tailcoat and neat striped trousers that James was wearing, "see how smart James is!"

And then they looked at the old knitted cardigan and baggy trousers that Charlie wore.

"And look, Our Charlie," they said, when James tossed his silver-handled cane in the air and caught it. "What a clever chap your cousin is."

And then they looked as Charlie threw his wooden stick with string tied round the handle in the air and it crashed to the ground when he tried to catch it.

And when they had the barn dance on Saturday night, all the animals admired James. "What a wonderful dancer your cousin is," they said, as Charlie kept tripping over his feet.

And when they had a party for

James, all the animals said, "Your cousin can do anything, Our Charlie, he dresses well, he dances well and he plays the piano well. You're lucky having a cousin like that."

And then they all said, "Three cheers for James! The pig who can do anything!"

And when it was time for James to go back to his little house in the middle of the town, Charlie said, "I wish I was like you. I wish I could look like you, and twirl my stick like you, and dance like you and play the piano like you. I can't do anything."

"Come and stay with me," said James, "and I'll teach you."

So Charlie went to stay with James until he could dress like

James, twirl a cane like James, dance like James and play the piano like James.

And when he went back to the farm, all the animals said, "Where's Our Charlie? We miss him."

"I'm Charlie," said Charlie. "I'm wearing new clothes."

And all the animals looked at the black shiny top hat and the long tailcoat and smart striped trousers with neat creases in them.

"But we liked your old clothes," they said.

"I can do tricks with my new silver-topped cane," said Charlie, and he threw it in the air and caught it before it hit the ground.

"But we liked it when you

dropped your wooden stick with the string handle," they said.

"I can dance," said Charlie.

"But we liked you when you tripped over your feet," they said.

"I can play the piano," he said.

"We liked you when you couldn't," said the animals. "We liked Our Charlie the way he was."

"Good," said Charlie, "because these clothes are uncomfortable, and I like my wooden stick with the string round the handle, and dancing makes my feet hurt and I don't much like playing the piano."

So Charlie changed into his old clothes, and picked up his wooden stick with string on the handle.

Then all the animals said, "Three cheers for Our Charlie, hip hip hooray . . ."

And Charlie did a little dance, and fell over.

"Hip hip hooray," they cheered, "hip hip hooray for Charlie."

A Little Bit of Colour

Nancy Blishen

Thomas and Daniel were best
friends. Thomas was just over
five and Daniel was just over five
and a half. Daniel's extra half was
important when they had to decide
who would choose what games to
play, or who would sit next to the
driver on the school bus.

"I'm half a year older than you,
so *I* can choose," Daniel would say.

Their parents were best friends,
too; and that is why the two
families lived together in a big, old
house. Thomas and his family lived

in the flat upstairs, and Daniel and his parents lived downstairs. The boys thought the best thing about the house was that it had a cellar where they played when the weather was bad, and where they could make as much mess as they liked and not get into trouble. There was also a big garden with an orchard full of apple and pear and plum trees, a stable and an old, rather broken-down greenhouse.

It was the last week of the summer holidays. Thomas and Daniel had been to the seaside for two weeks. They had made a den in the cellar, and a camp in the orchard. They had played pirates, and cowboys and Red Indians, crusaders, and explorers. They'd done all the things children love to do in the holidays. Now it was almost time for school to begin again, and they had to think quite hard to find things to do to keep themselves happy.

Then one sunny morning, Daniel woke up and a wonderful idea popped into his head. He couldn't wait to finish his breakfast so he could go and tell Thomas about it. They ran down into the garden and Daniel said, "Tom, why don't we paint the greenhouse? Not white like it is now, but all the colours of the rainbow!"

"But what would our mums and dads say?" said Thomas, looking worried.

"Oh, that's all right," said Daniel. "I heard my dad say . . ."

11

And he whispered in Thomas's ear.

"Great!" said Thomas, and they went into the cellar to collect paint and brushes. On a shelf they found a row of half-empty paint tins – blue, green, orange, yellow and red. They carried these down to the greenhouse and started work.

"Let's paint the doors orange and the window frames blue with yellow edges," said Thomas.

"My favourite colour's red," said Daniel, "so I'm going to have red windows with green edges."

They were so happy and excited that they didn't notice that not all the paint was finishing up on the greenhouse. But then Thomas caught sight of himself in a window pane.

"Hey, Dan, look! I'm the Terrible Monster with Orange Hair!"

Then Daniel peered at himself in the glass. His face was covered with paint spots.

"I'm the Green-Spotted Monster!" he giggled.

Suddenly a window in the upstairs flat opened and Thomas's mother called out.

"Boys, would you like orange juice and a chocolate biscuit? We're coming out—"

"Yes, *please*!" they shouted together.

"Do you think they'll like the new greenhouse?" whispered Daniel.

"Of course they will," said Thomas. "It looks *much* better!" And they stood back and admired

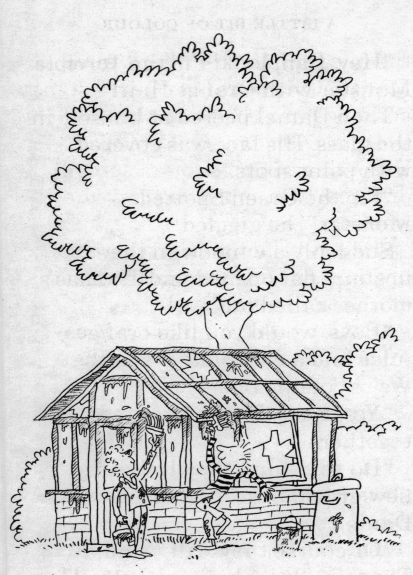

the effect of all their hard work.

At that moment they heard steps coming down the path. But suddenly the footsteps stopped. Daniel's mother let out a scream and nearly dropped the tray she was carrying.

"Danny, what on earth have you been doing? Look at your *face* . . . and your *jeans* . . . and the *greenhouse*! What will Daddy say?"

Thomas's mother was coming down the path behind her.

"I *thought* they were very quiet," she said.

"It's all right," said Daniel. "Daddy will be pleased. I know he will. I heard him say last week, 'What this garden needs is a bit of *colour*!'"

"But he didn't mean *paint* – he

15

meant *flowers*!" said Daniel's mother. But she didn't sound *quite* so cross.

"Oh," said Thomas and Daniel, looking at each other. Then they looked at their mothers. Their shoulders seemed to be shaking, and funny bubbly noises were coming from inside them. Suddenly they were all laughing helplessly – both mothers *and* Thomas *and* Daniel.

Thomas's mother was the first to recover.

"OK, boys," she said. "We'll forgive you this time. But don't ever do anything like that again without asking first. And now let's get the paint off your hands and we can have tea."

After a lot of scrubbing, which

hurt a bit, the two boys were back in the orchard with their drinks and biscuits.

"Dad is funny," said Daniel. "How was I to know that he meant flowers?"

"Well," said Thomas, "what do you think *my* dad said yesterday? I heard him talking to Mr Black next door, and he said, 'We're lucky to be living here and not in a box in a row of other little boxes.' Now, what do you think he meant by *that*?"

"I dunno," said Daniel. "But it might have been fun to live in a box. Don't you think so, Tom?"

"Except when it rained," said Thomas.

And the idea made them laugh so much that they forgot they

didn't quite know what their dads would say when they came home that evening and discovered the Rainbow Greenhouse.

Philibert the First

Dick King-Smith

Felicia was a wonderful country. Every Monday was a Bank Holiday and no one worked on a day with an S in it (which just left Friday).

It never rained in the daytime but only at night.

There were no traffic problems because everyone rode about (very slowly) on donkeys.

And there were no schools. If you wanted to know something, you asked your mum or dad, and if they didn't know how many beans make five, then neither would you.

Finally, even if they didn't always actually love their neighbours, Felicians were always nice to one another, so that everyone was happy. Except the King.

King Philibert the First of Felicia had everything anyone could want. He had his health and strength, he had a beautiful wife and three handsome sons and three pretty daughters, and a magnificent palace and loads of servants and pots of money and a pet walrus called Norman. What more could any man desire?

Yet King Philibert had become unhappy and not a single Felician knew the reason why, not even the Queen.

"Philibert," she would say each day. "Why are you unhappy?" And each day the King would reply, "I'm sorry, my dear, but I do not know."

"You do still love me, don't you?" the Queen would say, and the King would answer "Yes, my dear, I do," but oh, how sadly he said it.

It was the same with the little princes and princesses. On Fridays those that could read studied the *Encyclopaedia Felicianica* and those that could only weed worked in the Palace gardens. But on every other day they too asked their father, "Why are you unhappy, Papa?" and the King would reply, "I'm sorry, my children, I wish I knew why."

Everyone else wished so too,

21

because all of them, right down to
the poorest beggar in the streets of
the capital, FeliCity, were as
happy as larks, while their King
was as miserable as sin, with a
face as long as a boot.

Only one living creature in
Felicia looked as sad as King
Philibert, and that was his pet
walrus, Norman.

Norman was twelve feet long and
so fat that he weighed a ton and a
half. Some Felicians on an
expedition to Greenland had
brought him back as a fiftieth
birthday present for the King.

Norman's favourite food was
oysters, and every morning King
Philibert would feed him dozens of
them (except when there was an R
in the month, and then Norman

had to make do with mussels).

And every morning the King would pat the walrus on top of his huge round bald head, and say sadly, "There, was that nice?" and in reply Norman would give a deep gurgly moan that sounded like "Gloom!" Then the King and his pet walrus would stare sorrowfully at one another, the very picture of unhappiness.

"I never can decide," said the Queen to the little princes and princesses, "which looks the more miserable."

She had of course often consulted the Royal Doctor about the King's condition, but though he had suggested dieting, and exercise, and hot and cold baths, and even taking the day off on

Fridays, nothing had worked. Even the Court Jester's funniest jokes could raise no smile on the face of King Philibert the First of Felicia.

One morning as the King finished feeding his walrus with the oysters, he said with a sigh, "Very soon, Norman, I shall be fifty-one, and then it will be a whole year since first you arrived and since last I smiled."

"Gloom!" answered Norman.

And gloom there was, a day or so later, for the walrus was suddenly taken ill with the stomach-ache. To the one usual word he spoke was added another.

"Doom!" moaned Norman. "Doom!"

Feeling sadder than ever, the King sent for the Royal Vet.

Now it so happened that the Royal Vet was newly appointed and had never before set eyes on King Philibert, let alone on Norman.

"What seems to be the trouble, Your Majesty?" he asked politely.

"It's Norman," said the King sadly. "He has the tummy-ache, poor fellow. This morning he actually refused his food."

"What food, Sire?" asked the Royal Vet.

"Oysters, of course."

"In the second week of May?" said the Royal Vet.

"Oh help!" said King Philibert. "I was thinking it was still April. There's no R in this month."

"Exactly," said the Royal Vet. "No wonder he has the tummy-ache."

"Doom!" groaned Norman.

"We'll soon put him right," said the Royal Vet. "Starve him for a couple of days and then switch to mussels and he'll be as right as rain."

The King sighed.

The Royal Vet looked carefully at his royal master.

"Forgive me, Sire," he said, "if I

say that you do not look as happy
as the average Felician. In fact you
do not look at all happy. In fact
you look downright wretched."

"I am," said King Philibert.
"Soon it will be a year since last I
smiled."

The Royal Vet looked extremely
thoughtful.

"How long, may I ask," he said,
"has Your Majesty kept this
walrus as a pet?"

"Almost a year," said the King.
"He was a fiftieth birthday present
and soon I shall be fifty-one."

"That's it!" cried the Royal Vet.

"That's what?" cried the King.

"Gloom!" moaned the walrus.

"Norman," said the Royal Vet,
"is the cause of Your Majesty's
unhappiness. Looking at Norman's

gloomy face has made you gloomy too."

"Must I get rid of him then?" said the King. "Must Norman go?"

"No, no, Sire," said the Royal Vet. "What we must do is to turn Norman into a happy walrus, and I think I know how to do this."

"How?" asked the King.

"Leave it to me, Your Majesty," said the Royal Vet.

So King Philibert left it to him.

Thus it was that, some months later, another expedition arrived back from Greenland with another present for the King.

It was another walrus, much like Norman to look at, but smaller. When he saw it, King Philibert looked even sadder than usual.

"If one walrus makes me

miserable," he said, "what will two do?"

But Norman didn't look sadder than usual. Norman didn't look as sad as usual. Norman didn't look sad at all.

His dull fishy eyes suddenly lit up at the sight of the new walrus, his moustache bristled, his mournful expression turned into a kind of a grin. Then he opened his mouth and out of it came, not the usual "Gloom!" or "Doom!" but a happy excited roaring noise that sounded like "Vroom! Vroom!" as he lumbered forward to touch noses with the newcomer.

"He likes him," said King Philibert.

"He likes her, you mean," said the Royal Vet.

"Oh," said the King. "I see. You mean . . .?"

"I mean, Your Majesty," said the Royal Vet, "that from now on Norman will be a different animal. Just look at him!"

And King Philibert looked at his happy walrus, and a great smile spread over his face. Then he began to chuckle, and then he began to laugh, so loudly that the Queen and the three little princes

and the three little princesses and
all the members of the Royal
Household came running to see
what on earth had happened.

Oh, what joy there was throughout
the land of Felicia as the glad
news of the King's recovery
became known!

Happy as the people had thought
themselves before, now they were
even happier, especially when they
learned that in celebration a Royal
Decree had been issued,
forbidding anyone to work on
Fridays.

"Oh, Philibert!" said the Queen
when at last they were alone
together. "You do still love me,
don't you?"

"Yes, my dear," said King

31

Philibert the First of Felicia. "I am very, very glad to say I do. Without the shadow of a doubt we shall live happily ever after."

And they did.

Mrs Goat and her Seven Little Kids

Written and illustrated by Tony Ross

Once upon a time, Big Mother
Goat was about to go to the
supermarket.

"Kids," she said to her children,
"don't you open that door to
anyone. If you do, the hungry wolf
will probably get in, and eat you
all. Now, we don't want that, do
we?"

"No, we don't want that," said
the kids.

"I'll kick him on the leg,"

shouted the littlest one.

Now the wolf was hiding underneath the window, and he heard all this. When Big Mother Goat had gone on her way, he knocked on the door.

"Who's that?" shouted the kids together.

"I'm your mum," the wolf growled. "Open up the door, I forgot to give you your pocket money."

"You're not Mum," shouted the littlest one. "Mum's got a squeaky little voice that sounds like music."

"You're the Hungry Wolf," shouted the kids, and they wouldn't open the door.

So the wolf ran off to the music teacher's house.

"Teach me to speak in a squeaky little voice, like music," he growled. "If you don't, I'll bite your beak off."

"Very well," said the music teacher, and she did her best.

Then the wolf hurried back to the kids' house, and banged on the door. "Let me in, this is Mummy, I've got some sweets for you," he called.

"Show us your hoof first," said the littlest one, and the wolf pushed his paw through the letterbox.

"That's not Mum's hoof," cried the kids. "Mum's hoof's white. You're the Hungry Wolf."

The littlest one hit the paw with his little hammer, and the kids refused to open the door.

"OWWWWWWCHHHH!" The wolf snatched his paw out of the letterbox, and sucked his fingers. "White, is it?" he snarled, and went off to find an artist.

"It's got to be white, with a little black bit at the end, just like a goat's hoof," he told the artist. "Make a good job of it, and I'll not bite your nose off."

The artist made a very good job

of it, and the wolf hurried back to the house where the kids lived.

He banged on the door, and shouted in a squeaky little voice, like music, "Let me in, dearies. I've brought you some comics from the supermarket." The wolf waved his paw through the letterbox. "Look, it's Mummy."

"It's Mum's hoof all right," said one of the kids.

"And it's Mum's little squeaky voice like music," said another. "Open the door."

"Not so fast . . ." said the littlest one. "Let's see your tail."

The wolf stuck his tail through the letterbox.

"Mum's tail is dainty, like an ear of wheat," said one kid. "This tail is grey and bushy, like . . . like . . ."

"Like the Hungry's Wolf's tail," cried the littlest one. "Excuse me while I bite it."

The wolf howled, and the kids refused to open the door.

"So Mum's tail is dainty, like an ear of wheat, is it?" muttered the wolf, and he rushed off to see the dentist.

"I don't usually remove tails," said the dentist.

"If you don't remove this one, I'll bite your tail off," said the wolf.

"Then I'll make an exception in your case," said the dentist. "After all, I do have the necessary equipment. This'll not hurt."

The wolf stuck an ear of wheat where his tail was, and once again banged on the kids' front door.

"Let me in," he cried, in his little squeaky voice like music, waving his paw painted like a hoof. "I'm Mummy, and I've got ice cream."

He turned round, and wiggled his new tail.

"It's Mum's little voice, squeaky, like music," said one kid.

"It's Mum's hoof, white with a little black tip," said another.

"It's Mum's tail, dainty, like an ear of wheat," said a third.

"It's Mum!" they all shouted joyfully, and threw open the door. All that is, except the littlest one, who wasn't so sure, so he hopped into the coal bucket to hide.

In leaped the wolf, and swallowed six little kids whole.

"I thought there were seven," grumbled the wolf. "Seven would have been delicious. Still, six is OK."

So saying, he loosened his belt, and helped himself to a glass of Big Mother Goat's best beer.

The wolf took the beer into the back garden, and sat down in a wicker chair. Then, with an awful grin on his face, he dozed in the sun.

When Big Mother Goat got home, she was laden down with seven bags of sweets, seven comics, and seven ice creams.

The littlest one jumped out of the coal bucket and told his mother exactly what had happened.

"He's still here, Mum," he bleated. "He's in the garden. He's in your chair."

"WHAT?" roared Big Mother Goat, dropping all her bags. "In my chair? With my kids in him? LET ME GET AT HIM!"

Big Mother Goat hit the dozing wolf at ninety miles an hour.

She butted him right out of the wicker chair.

She butted him so hard, that one of her kids shot out of his mouth.

She butted him again, and out came another.

"Not again!" pleaded the wolf, trying to crawl away. "Not on my bottom, my tail place still hurts . . . OW!"

She butted him again, and out flew a third kid.

Altogether, Big Mother Goat butted the wolf seven times. Once

each to get back her six swallowed children, and once to send the wolf right over the trees, and away for ever.

Then she gathered her kids around her, dried their tears, and gave each one a big kiss on the nose . . . and a slap on the ear for opening the door to a wolf.

Maggie McMuddle and the Chocolate Cake

Moira Miller

There were some days when Maggie McMuddle just could not make her mind up about anything. If she went to the supermarket to buy a tin of soup, she would ask everyone she met what they liked best and end up either buying six tins or none at all.

One afternoon she found a recipe

in a magazine for a particularly beautiful chocolate cake.

"Lovely and dark, with lots of thick butter icing in the middle, and some on top," said Maggie McMuddle. "Just the ticket for tea-time, Purpuss."

"Hmmm," said Purpuss. He was not all that fond of chocolate cake really, but he was always happy when the oven was on to do some baking, because then the old draughty kitchen was so much cosier.

Maggie McMuddle took out her big blue and white baking bowl, and went to the larder cupboard.

"Sugar, margarine, cocoa powder," she counted out the packets. "Two brown eggs, and flour."

But there was no flour.

"Oh, foozle!" said Maggie McMuddle as she searched through the cupboard. "I remember now. I finished it when I made the scones. I'll just have to toot down to the supermarket for some more. There's plenty of time."

She popped her nose out of the front door to see what the weather was doing. It was a winter day, but crisp and bright and sunny.

"Don't need a coat," she said, and pulled on her big woolly cardigan. Then she picked up her shopping bag, took the key from the hook by the door, and off she went.

Mr Brown next door was slowly raking up leaves in his front garden.

"Trees," he muttered. "Nasty messy things, leaves falling all over the place." He picked a fallen leaf off one of the ducks cut in his front hedge.

"Afternoon," said Maggie McMuddle. "Lovely day for the time of year, don't you think?"

Mr Brown stopped what he was doing, straightened up, and looked around him gloomily. "Well," he said slowly. "It might be at the moment, but just you wait until the sun goes behind a cloud. Chilly wind that, chilly wind."

"Oh dear, do you really think so?" Maggie McMuddle shivered, feeling colder already. "Perhaps I'd better go back for my warm coat after all."

"I should," said Mr Brown,

getting back to his raking. "You can never be too careful."

Maggie McMuddle went back up the path, scrabbling about in the bottom of her bag for the key. She let herself in and pulled on her thick winter coat. Purpuss watched her lazily. The coat only just buttoned up on top of the cardigan.

"My, that's cosy. Feels better already," she said, picking up her bag and setting off again.

"'Bye Mr Brown."

"'Bye Mrs M."

At the corner of the street, outside his dad's café, Sandy Sullivan was polishing his motorbike.

"Afternoon Sandy. Nice day – if a teensy bit chilly, don't you think?"

"Haaa," said Sandy, breathing on the silver metal, and rubbing hard with his duster. "Bound to rain."

"Oh, surely not," said Mrs McMuddle.

"Always does when I polish the bike," said Sandy, giving a final rub to the mirror. "Look at those clouds, they're all sitting up there waiting till I'm finished."

"I see what you mean," said Mrs McMuddle. There were just a few small grey clouds drifting across the sky. "Perhaps I'd better just take a raincoat after all."

She hurried off back home, rummaging through her bag and pockets for the front door key. At last she found it, and let herself in. Purpuss looked a little

surprised as she pulled on her
pink plastic raincoat over the
winter coat and tried to fasten the
poppers. Each time she bent to do
the bottom one, the top ones
pinged open again.

"Oof, this coat is getting a little
bit tight," she gasped. "Perhaps I
need a new one."

She picked up her bag, shut the
door and set off again.

"'Bye Mr Brown."

"'Bye Mrs M."

"Goodbye Sandy."

"Toodle-oo, Auntie Mac."

Round the corner she went, and
along to the crossing at the park
gates. A painter was busy at work
on the railings.

"Nice afternoon," said Mrs
McMuddle. "A wee bit cold, and it

might rain, but it's really rather pleasant."

"A *wee* bit cold!" said the painter. "I've been working on these railings all afternoon. Haven't had a tea-break yet, Missus, and I'm frozen! It's cold enough for snow if you ask me."

"Snow!" Mrs McMuddle was in a real tizzy. "Oh dear, that would fairly ruin my good shoes. I think I'd better just slip home and change into my wellington boots."

So back she hurried. Past the painter, past Sandy Sullivan, polishing his bike, and Mr Brown slowly raking the leaves in his garden. Back up her own front path, rummaging in her bag, and through all her pockets.

"Drat that key, where does it get

to?" At last she found it, let herself in and sat down, puffing and gasping to pull on her wellington boots. Purpuss stood up and walked round in a circle on his toes, with his legs stiff, just to show that he was a little annoyed at being woken up again.

"I can hardly see my feet," puffed Maggie McMuddle. "Never mind

pull my boots on. Just as well I don't have to tie laces." At the front door she turned back and added a warm hat and a scarf.

"Just to be sure," she said, looking at herself in the hall mirror. "Now the weather can do what it likes, I'm ready for anything." She squeezed through the front door and off down the path.

"'Bye Mr Brown."

"'Bye Mrs M."

"Goodbye Sandy."

"Toodle-oo."

"Goodbye painter. I hope you feel warmer soon."

"Tara, luv. Should do, I'm clocking off in ten minutes."

Opposite the park gate, PC Peters was on traffic duty. She smiled and nodded. Mrs

McMuddle waited until all the cars stopped, and then she stepped off the pavement to cross to the supermarket.

"Lovely day, isn't it?" said PC Peters. "Just like spring again." Mrs McMuddle stopped, right there in the middle of the road and stared up at her.

"Oh! Do you really think so?" she said. "You don't think it's a wee bit cold?"

"I'm warm enough!"

"Or that it might rain?"

"Rain? No chance!"

"Or snow even?"

"Never!" laughed PC Peters. "It's a lovely day."

"Um – oh dear," Mrs McMuddle looked at the supermarket across the road, then she turned back.

"Back in a tick," she called, leaving PC Peters to sort out all the traffic.

She hurried back up Antimacassar Street, past the painter, past Sandy Sullivan, still polishing his motorbike, past Mr Brown raking up the last of the leaves.

She puffed up the front path, frantically searching for her key.

"I know I had it when I came out. It was in my bag. No, maybe I put it in my raincoat pocket, or in my heavy coat pocket, or my cardigan . . ." She found it at last, and let herself in.

Purpuss completely ignored her.

"Oof," she gasped, pulling off her boots, raincoat, scarf, hat and the heavy winter coat. "That feels much better. I knew it was going to be a nice day. Now I'd better hurry if I'm going to get to the shops on time."

And off she set once more. No Mr Brown, he had finished dusting his front path and gone indoors. No Sandy, he was sitting in the café, with a mug of tea, admiring his shiny bike. Round the corner, past the park, there was a WET PAINT sign on the railing, but the painter had gone. Along to the crossing, and PC Peters had gone off duty. Mrs McMuddle waited until the road was clear and then trotted across to the supermarket, just in time to see the manager putting up the CLOSED sign.

"Oh bother!" she said. "I've left it too late. That's what comes of letting other people make up your mind for you, and I was so looking forward to that chocolate cake, too."

"I am sorry, madam," said the manager. "Was it something special you wanted?"

"Flour," said Maggie McMuddle, following him back into the shop before he had a chance to close the door. "I was going to do some baking, but I found that I'd run out of flour . . ."

The manager put his glasses on the end of his nose and began to hunt along the shelves.

"and then I met Mr Brown, and he said it was going to be cold, so I had to go back for my warm coat . . ."

"Self-raising or plain?" said

the manager.

"Plain . . . but then when I met Sandy Sullivan, he thought it might rain – well it did look a bit like it at the time . . ."

"White or wholemeal?"

"White, please . . . and then the painter at the park said it felt like snow. Well, really I said, but I had to go back and change into my boots, just in case. Better safe than sorry . . ."

"Large or small?"

"Large . . . and PC Peters said it was just like spring, and there was me, all wrapped up like a Christmas parcel. That's lovely, dear, just pop it in my bag and I'll toddle off home now."

"Good thing you caught me in time," said the manager as Maggie

McMuddle counted out the right money.

"That's true. I might not have been able to bake my cake, and it's all my own silly fault for allowing other people to change my mind once I've made it up. I won't do it again. Not ever."

"Very wise, madam," said the manager, letting her out. "What sort of cake is it?"

"Chocolate of course, with lots of thick butter icing. That's my favourite."

"Really?" said the manager, locking the door behind them. "I prefer cherry cake myself. All that lovely juicy fruit. Mmmm!"

Maggie McMuddle waved as he walked off down the road, then she looked both ways, very carefully, and crossed to the park gates.

"Cherry cake? Well," she thought as she walked past the railings and turned the corner into Antimacassar Street.

"Haven't had one of those for a long time. Make a nice change from chocolate," she thought as she passed the corner café.

"I don't know . . ." she said to herself. She waved to Mr Brown who was standing in his front window staring gloomily out into the garden at the leaves blowing down from the trees across the road.

"Maybe I will . . ." She rummaged in the bottom of her bag for the front door key.

"But I wonder if I've got enough cherries . . .?"

Mrs Pepperpot Minds the Baby

Alf Prøysen

Mrs Pepperpot has a strange problem – she's never sure when she is going to shrink to the size of a pepperpot! This can cause a few problems, especially when there are full-size babies on the loose!

Now I'll tell you what happened the day Mrs Pepperpot was asked to mind the baby.

Mrs Pepperpot was asleep in bed

when suddenly there was a knock at the door. She looked at the clock. "Good heavens!" she cried. "Have I slept so long?" She pulled her clothes on very quickly and ran to open the door.

In the porch stood a lady with a little boy on her arm.

"Forgive me for knocking," said the lady.

"You're welcome," said Mrs Pepperpot.

"You see," said the lady, "I'm staying with my aunt near here with my little boy, and today we simply *have* to go shopping in the town. I can't take Roger and there's no one in the house to look after him."

"Oh, that's all right!" said Mrs Pepperpot. "I'll look after your

little boy." (To herself she thought,
However will I manage with all
that work and me oversleeping like
that. Ah well, I shall have to do
both at the same time.) Then she
said out loud, "Roger, come to Mrs
Pepperpot? That's right!" And she
took the baby from the lady.

"You don't need to give him a
meal," said the lady. "I've brought
some apples for him, for when he
starts sucking his fingers."

"Very well," said Mrs Pepperpot,
and put the apples in a dish on the
sideboard.

The lady said goodbye and Mrs
Pepperpot set the baby down on
the rug in the sitting room. Then
she went out into the kitchen
to fetch her broom to start
sweeping up. At that very moment

she *shrank*!

"Oh dear! Oh dear! Whatever shall I do?" she wailed, for of course now she was much smaller than the baby. She gave up any idea of cleaning the house.

I must go and see what that little fellow is doing, she thought, as she climbed over the doorstep into the sitting room.

Not a moment too soon! For Roger had crawled right across the floor and was just about to pull the tablecloth off the table together with a pot of jam, a loaf of bread, and a big jug of coffee!

Mrs Pepperpot lost no time. She knew it was too far for her to get to the table, so she pushed over a large silver cup which was standing on the floor, waiting to be polished. Her husband had won it in a skiing competition years ago when he was young.

The cup made a fine booming noise as it fell; the baby turned round and started crawling towards it.

"That's right," said Mrs Pepperpot, "you play with that; at least you can't break it."

But Roger wasn't after the silver cup. Gurgling, "Ha' dolly! Ha' dolly!" he made a bee-line for Mrs Pepperpot, and before she could get away, he had grabbed her by the waist! He jogged her up and down and every time Mrs Pepperpot kicked and wriggled to get free, he laughed. "'Ickle, 'ickle!" he shouted, for she was tickling his hand with her feet.

"Let go! Let go!" yelled Mrs Pepperpot. But Roger was used to his father shouting "Let's go!" when he threw him up in the air and caught him again. So Roger shouted "Leggo! Leggo!" and threw the little old woman up in the air with all the strength of his short arms.

Mrs Pepperpot went up and

down – nearly to the ceiling! Luckily she landed on the sofa, but she bounced several times before she could stop.

"Talk of flying through the air with the greatest of ease!" she gasped. "If that had happened to me in my normal size I'd most likely have broken every bone in my body. Ah well, I'd better see what my little friend is up to now."

She soon found out. Roger had got hold of a matchbox and was trying to strike a match. Luckily he was using the wrong side of the box, but Mrs Pepperpot had to think very quickly indeed.

"Youngsters like to copy everything you do, so I'll take this nut and throw it at him. Then he'll throw it at me – I hope."

She had found the nut in the sofa
and now she was in such a hurry
to throw it she forgot to aim
properly. But it was a lucky shot
and it hit Roger just behind the
ear, making him turn round.
"What else can I throw?"
wondered Mrs Pepperpot, but
there was no need, because the
baby had seen her; he dropped the
matchbox and started crawling
towards the sofa.

"Ha' dolly! Ha' dolly!" he
gurgled delightedly.

And now they started a very
funny game of hide-and-seek – at
least it was fun for Roger, but not
quite so amusing for poor little old
Mrs Pepperpot who had to hide
behind the cushions to get away
from him. In the end she managed

to climb onto the sideboard where she kept a precious geranium in a pot.

"Aha, you can't catch me now!" she said, feeling much safer.

But at that moment the baby decided to go back to the matchbox. "No, no, no!" shouted Mrs Pepperpot. Roger took no notice. So, when she saw he was trying to strike another match, she put her back against the flowerpot and gave it a push so that it fell to the floor with a crash.

Roger immediately left the matchbox for this new and interesting mess of earth and bits of broken flowerpot. He buried both his hands in it and started putting it in his mouth, gurgling, "Nice, din-din!"

"No, no, no!" shouted Mrs Pepperpot once more. "Oh, whatever shall I do?" Her eye caught the apples left by Roger's mother. They were right beside her on the dish. One after the other she rolled them over the edge of the dish onto the floor. Roger watched them roll, then he decided to chase them, forgetting his lovely meal of earth and broken flowerpot. Soon the apples were all over the floor and the baby was crawling happily from one to the other.

There was a knock on the door.

"Come in," said Mrs Pepperpot.

Roger's mother opened the door and came in, and there was Mrs Pepperpot as large as life.

"Has he been naughty?" asked

the lady.

"As good as gold," said Mrs Pepperpot. "We've had a high old time together, haven't we, Roger?" And she handed him back to his mother.

"I'll have to take you home now, Precious," said the lady.

But the little fellow began to cry. "Ha' dolly! Ha' dolly!" he sobbed.

"Have *dolly*?" said his mother. "But you didn't bring a dolly – you don't even have one at home." She turned to Mrs Pepperpot. "I don't know what he means."

"Oh, children say so many things grown-ups don't understand," said Mrs Pepperpot, and waved goodbye to Roger and his mother.

Then she set about cleaning up her house.

Betsey's Birthday Surprise

Malorie Blackman

The moment Betsey opened her eyes, she expected wonderful, sun-shiny, brilliant surprises. Well, she got a surprise all right! A nasty surprise. A *horrible* surprise. Everyone had forgotten her birthday!

At first Betsey couldn't believe it. Botheration! How could everyone have forgotten that today was her birthday?

"Gran'ma Liz, guess what today

is?" Betsey asked hopefully.

"Saturday," said Gran'ma Liz. "Now run along and play, Betsey. I've got things to do."

Betsey decided to give Gran'ma Liz a teeny-tiny clue.

"Gran'ma, haven't you forgotten something?" Betsey asked. "Something wonderful about the day and *me*."

If Gran'ma Liz didn't get it from that then she didn't deserve to call herself a gran'ma!

"Betsey child, what are you talking about? It's Saturday. That's it! End of story! And . . ." Gran'ma Liz slapped her hand against her forehead. "I'd forget my head if it wasn't glued to my neck! Thanks for reminding me, Betsey. I promised your mam I'd make some

of her favourite biscuits for when
she comes home from work. I'd
better get started."

"But . . . but . . ." That's not what
Betsey meant at all!

"D'you want to help me?" asked
Gran'ma Liz.

No way! Not today of all days. It
looked like Gran'ma Liz really *had*
forgotten. Betsey wandered out
into the backyard. Sherena bowled
a cricket ball to Desmond who hit
it into the dirt.

"Why the glum face, Betsey?"
asked Sherena as she picked up
the ball.

"Because today is . . . today is . . ."

"A kind of nothing day," Sherena
finished Betsey's sentence. "I
know exactly what you mean.
There's nothing special going on.

74

There's nothing to see, nothing to do. And it's the kind of day when you don't want to do anything either."

Betsey really couldn't believe it. All week she'd reminded everyone that it was her birthday on Saturday and they'd still forgotten. How *could* they? Even May hadn't sent a card. Betsey felt tears prick at her eyes.

"Sherena, I can't practise hitting the ball if you don't throw it to me," Desmond called out from the other end of the backyard.

"D'you want to stay and play cricket with us?" Sherena asked Betsey. "You can be the wicket keeper if you like."

"Stuff the wicket keeper!" Betsey snapped.

"Charming!" Sherena raised her eyebrows as Betsey flounced back into the house.

So it was true. They had all forgotten. Maybe Mam hadn't – but she wasn't here. But the rest had! There were no cards, no presents. And forget about a birthday cake! There wasn't even a birthday sandwich! Betsey would've settled for a birthday biscuit!

"Then I'll just have to do something on my own!" Betsey muttered.

Yeah! That's what she'd do. She'd celebrate her own birthday – all by herself. She'd show them all. She needed to do something fun to cheer herself up. Something *different*!

"I know!" Betsey clapped her hands.

She marched into Mam and Dad's bedroom. She switched on Mam's radio to listen to some dance music. That would cheer her up for a start. Then Betsey sat at the dressing-table and picked up Mam's most expensive bottle of perfume. Dad had bought it especially for her the last time he came home.

"I have to smell nice on my birthday," Betsey mumbled. She squirted some on her wrists . . . and her neck . . . and her feet and her legs . . . and her arms . . . and reached around to squirt some up and down her back. That was more like it! Betsey looked over the dressing-table. What next? Make-up! That would make her look better – more like a birthday girl.

"I have to look good on my birthday," Betsey decided.

Very carefully, Betsey put on some of Mam's lipstick. Next she tried some of Mam's eye-shadow. She wasn't sure about the eye-shadow but she left it on.

What now? Betsey spotted the

very thing. She opened Mam's jewellery box and put on a pair of Mam's long, dangly earrings and her matching long, dangly necklace.

"I have to sparkle on my birthday!" Betsey smiled at herself in the dressing-table mirror.

"Clothes!" Betsey announced. "That's what I need!"

She definitely needed some birthday clothes. She opened Mam and Dad's wardrobe. She saw the very thing. Mam's favourite black dress. Betsey pulled it off the hanger. She slipped off her own clothes and put on Mam's dress. It only reached to Mam's knees when she wore it but on Betsey it trailed on to the floor. It didn't look *too* bad though.

"Perfect! Now I really do look like a birthday girl," Betsey said, admiring herself in the mirror. "I think I'd better turn off the radio. I don't want anyone to come in until I've finished."

"Betsey, could you come here for a second?" Gran'ma Liz called out.

"Coming," Betsey replied.

She tried to walk but tripped over the bottom of the dress. Betsey lifted up the hem and tried again. That was better! She opened the bedroom door and stepped out into the living-room.

"Gran'ma Liz, how do I loo . . . ?" Betsey's voice trailed off slowly.

"HAPPY BIRTHDAY, BETS . . ."

The living-room was full to

overflowing with Betsey's friends
and their parents. May was there –
and Josh and Celine and Martin.
Everyone was there. They'd all
started to wish Betsey a happy
birthday, but when they saw what
she was wearing, their voices
trailed off.

Betsey's voice had trailed off too.
She stared and stared, wondering
where all these people had
suddenly come from.

"Elizabeth Ruby Biggalow, I . . .
I . . ." For once Gran'ma Liz was
lost for words!

One or two people started to
titter. And three or four people
started to giggle. Then the whole
room erupted with laughter.

"Betsey, who told you to put on
my best dress? And what on earth

is that smell?" Mam choked.
"Child, you smell like a perfume
factory." And Mam marched
Betsey into the bathroom.

"Why are all my friends here?"
Betsey asked, amazed.

"Because I arranged a surprise
party for you," said Mam.

"A surprise party!" Betsey's eyes
gleamed. "For me?"

"You can rejoin it when I've got
all this muck off your face and
when you smell human again!"
said Mam.

Whilst the bath was running,
Mam stripped Betsey out of her
clothes. She washed Betsey's face
and scrubbed her body until
Betsey's skin felt piping hot. Then
Mam gave Betsey a box wrapped in
glittery paper.

"Happy birthday, Betsey," Mam smiled. "This is from your gran'ma and your dad and me."

Betsey tore off the paper in about two seconds flat. It was a dress. The most beautiful dress Betsey had ever seen. It was a deep blue silk, covered with tiny, delicate flowers. Betsey hugged Mam tight.

"Thanks, Mam," she said happily.

"Now isn't that better than my old black dress," Mam smiled as she led the way into the living-room.

As soon as everyone saw Betsey they all started clapping. They all agreed – Betsey looked wonderful.

"Well done, Betsey," grinned Uncle George. "We thought we'd surprise you with a party, but you had a surprise of your own!"

"It was my birthday surprise for all of you!" Betsey winked.

"I'm only sorry I forgot my camera at home!" laughed May's mam.

"Thank goodness you *did* forget it," sniffed Gran'ma Liz. "Otherwise we'd never have lived it down!"

But only Betsey heard that bit!

Secrets

Betsy Byars

Jimmy had never kept a secret in his life. Nobody would even tell him one any more. So far this year he had already told three.

The first secret was that his sister was getting a kitten for her birthday. He ran up the stairs so fast to tell her that he missed the last step. He fell flat on his face.

He jumped up. He threw open her door. He said, "Guess what you're getting for your birthday?" Before she could guess, he yelled, "A kitten!"

To his surprise his sister was not pleased. She even got mad. She yelled, "Mum! Jimmy told me what I'm getting. Now it won't be a surprise!"

When she got the kitten, the first thing she said to it was, "You were supposed to be a surprise, but Big Mouth told."

At Christmas he got another chance. "We're getting Mum new dishes," his sister said. "Now, don't tell!"

"I won't."

He ran into the kitchen. "I know what you're getting for Christmas."

"Don't tell," his mother said. "I like to be surprised."

"I won't tell." Then he couldn't help himself. He added, "But they're round and you eat off them."

"Jimmy!" his sister yelled.

When his mother opened the dishes, she said, "They are just beautiful."

His sister said, "But Big Mouth ruined the surprise."

It was like that all the time. He didn't want to tell. He just couldn't help himself.

At school he had ruined the birthday surprise party for Miss Brown. Miss Brown was called to the office, and while she was gone, one of the mothers had brought in a large box and hid it in the back of the room. When the teacher came in, Jimmy said, "Miss Brown! Miss Brown!"

"Yes, Jimmy."

"Someone left a box in the back of the room."

"Thank you, Jimmy, now get out your reading books."

"Miss Brown! Miss Brown!"

"Yes, Jimmy."

"It's a cake!"

No one would speak to Jimmy. At break one boy even hit him. "You told," he said. "You ruined the whole party." Jimmy dusted himself off and hung his head. He wished he had not told, but he couldn't help himself.

After that Jimmy was afraid no one would ever tell him a secret again. And he knew too that there was a secret going around his classroom. Just that morning when he came in, all the other kids stopped talking.

"What's up?" he asked his friend Roman.

Roman shrugged.

"Is it something I should know about?"

Roman said, "No."

That night Jimmy told his sister, "Everybody in my room knows a secret and they won't tell me."

"I don't blame them," said his sister.

"Why?"

"Because you blab. I know two secrets, and you would be the last person in the world I would tell."

"You know two secrets?"

"Yes."

"What are they?"

"No!"

"Just tell me one."

His sister left the room.

The next morning when Jimmy went to school he stopped outside the door. He listened. He heard someone say, "Shhhh! He's outside. He's listening. Don't give it away."

Everything got very quiet. Jimmy walked into the room and sat at his desk. In a low voice he said, "Please tell me the secret, Roman."

"No."

"I'd tell you."

"I know you would."

"Pleassssssssse!"

"Nnnnnoooooooo."

"Then I'll find out from somebody else."

After school he waited at the corner for Libby Rose. In Class One Libby had had trouble keeping a secret too. She had told that Rickie had a little snake in his pocket. Well, she had not actually told. She had said, "Mr Rogers, is it all right for us to bring snakes to school in our pockets?"

When he saw Libby, he said, "Libby, what's the big secret?"

Libby said, "I'm not telling."

"If I ever hear a secret, I'm not going to tell you."

"You're never going to hear one."

He followed Libby down the sidewalk on his knees. "Please please please please—"

"Oh, all right," Libby said. "Our teacher's going to get married."

He got up and dusted off his knees. He ran home like a cartoon character, leaving a streak behind him. He flung open the door. "I found out the secret! Our teacher's going to get married."

"She's already married," his mother said. "Somebody's teasing you."

That night he tried a desperate trick. He phoned Roman. "Well, I heard the big secret."

Roman said, "Did you?"

"Yes, so I guess it's no secret any more."

"I guess not."

"So we can talk about it, right?"

"Right. Who told you?"

Jimmy said, "First you tell me the secret so I can see if it's the same secret. Then I'll tell who told."

Roman said, "No deal."

"Just tell me one of the words in the secret."

But Roman hung up.

It was worse the next day. Jimmy was late for school. He could hear the class buzzing all the way down the corridor. He burst into the room. Silence. He decided to try another trick.

He said, "I heard you! I've been outside listening the whole time."

"Prove it," said Libby. "What did you hear?"

Jimmy stood there for a minute. Then he said, "Oh, nothing," and he went to his seat.

It was the longest secret in the world. It went on and on. Day after day, Jimmy would guess, "It's a party for somebody!" or, "The whole class is going to the zoo!" or, "We're going to give a play!" But he could tell from how happy his friends looked that he had not guessed right.

Finally Jimmy got tired of begging. When he came into the room on Monday and everyone was whispering, he just went to his seat. When he came into the room on Tuesday and they were whispering louder, he just went to his seat.

On Wednesday, only two girls

were whispering. Jimmy went to his seat. On Thursday, no one was whispering at all. Jimmy was glad about that. He went to his seat.

On Friday after school Roman surprised Jimmy. Roman said, "You want to know what the secret was?"

"Not any more," Jimmy said. "I've lost interest in secrets."

Roman said, "Then I'll tell you. The secret was that there was no secret."

"What?"

"The secret was that there was no secret. We just made you think there was one."

"There wasn't any secret?"

"There *was* a secret," Roman explained. "It was that there was no secret!"

"I *hate* that secret!"

"We knew you would."

"It's the worst secret I ever heard in my life! I hate that secret. Who thought of that terrible secret?"

"Everybody."

"Well, I hate it. I just hate it!"

"I do too," Roman said.

They started walking home. At the corner, Jimmy said, "You know, I think I'm cured."

Roman said, "What?"

"It's like having measles. You get over it, and you don't ever have it again. I had a bad case of secrets. Now I'm cured."

And his friend Roman said, "That's good."

Why's the Cow
on the Roof?

Robert Leeson

Ola and Kari made a splendid
couple, that's what everyone
said. He was tall and broad-
shouldered and hard working, she
was quick and cheerful.

They lived in a cottage right up
against the mountain with their
little baby, who crawled around
the kitchen floor and gurgled and
put things in its mouth to see what
they tasted like.

In the shed outside lived a brown

cow who supplied them with milk and cream, and behind the shed lived a black-and-white pig who was going to supply them with pork chops and bacon, but the pig didn't know that yet.

Every day Ola kissed Kari, took up his scythe and marched off to work in the fields while she got busy round the house. And when the sun was well over the mountain-top, Kari would walk up the valley and call Ola to come down and have his dinner. So it went on day after day. It couldn't be better. In fact, they ought to have lived happily ever after.

But there was just one thing wrong.

Now and then, Kari was a little late calling Ola for his dinner.

He'd come down to the cottage and find her sitting by the fire talking to the baby while she stirred the porridge in the pot.

"There you are, Ola," she would say. "Is that the time already? I've been so busy I forgot to come and call you."

Ola answered grumpily, "Busy doing what? I've mowed halfway down Ten Acre Meadow and you've just been sitting here watching the pot and playing with the baby. I'd love a job like that."

Kari smiled at him. "Oh, Ola, you have no idea how many things there are to do in the house. There's butter to churn for our dinner, the cow to feed and water, the kitchen to clean, the porridge to boil. And all the time I've got to watch the baby – and as for that pig, you need an eye on each finger to keep up with him."

"All that, eh?" said Ola. "And what do you do for the rest of the day? Read a book?"

Kari shook her head. "You don't know. The time goes – if it's not one thing, it's another. I hardly have a minute to turn round."

Ola was tired and grumpy and wouldn't be talked into a good mood. "Huh. I could do all that in half an hour, with one hand tied behind my back."

"Could you now?" Kari was beginning to get a little annoyed. But she changed her tone and put her arm around her husband's shoulder. "Look, let's not quarrel

101

over who does most work. Let's find out."

Ola was suspicious. "What does that mean?"

"Tomorrow we'll swap places. What d'you say? I'll go off haymaking and you stay home and look after the house. That way we'll see who works hardest."

"Why not?" Ola cheered up right away. "I like that idea." While he talked he was looking round the kitchen and working out how he would run the show, ha ha, and not have to slog up to Ten Acre Meadow and cut hay all day.

So they both went to bed in a good mood.

Early next morning Kari took the scythe over her shoulders and set off up the valley to join the haymakers. Ola waved her goodbye with a grin on his face and then got busy round the kitchen. Well begun is half done, everyone knows that. He'd soon have it sorted.

First he checked the baby was safe in the corner playing with its toys. Then he got cream from the dairy, poured it into the churn and began to swing the handle to turn it into butter.

After five minutes' hard churning he began to sweat. Take it easy, Ola, he told himself. No hurry. He opened the churn, but the butter wasn't set. So he started to churn again, a little more slowly.

By the time the butter was

nearly ready, so was he – for some light refreshment. Everything was going well – this job was a doddle. So he nipped down into the cellar for a drink of beer.

There was just one snag. The barrel hadn't been tapped. He looked round. Now which idiot had moved the mallet? Then he remembered. He'd used it yesterday and left it in the kitchen. Up the steps, quick look to see baby was happy, and then down into the cellar again. With a couple of sharp blows he knocked out the bung. Now he just had to fit the spigot into the hole and he could tap off a nice cool pint.

But as he stood with the spigot in one hand and the mallet in the other, he heard a strange scraping noise overhead. It didn't take him long to figure it out. The pig had sneaked into the kitchen.

He was halfway up the ladder when there was an almighty crash. He knew in a flash what it was – the pig had knocked over the churn! He was right. As he burst into the kitchen, cream and butter were running over the floor and the pig was lapping it up.

"You greedy swine!" yelled Ola and leaped across the room. The pig headed for the door, but not quickly enough. Rage gave Ola extra speed. He caught the black-and-white thief on the threshold and with one mighty kick stretched it out on the ground.

It didn't move. Ola looked down at it in dismay. Then he shrugged.

They were going to kill it later in the year anyway. First things first. Back to churning butter – for, being smart, he had left some cream in the dairy. He set to work again.

Then he stopped. Why was he standing here with the mallet in one hand and the spigot in the other? The beer barrel! Like a shot he was down in the cellar. But too late – the barrel had run dry. The kitchen floor ran with cream, the cellar floor with beer.

Back upstairs went Ola to churn more butter. He'd have to wait a while for his drink. Still, there were always teething problems.

But, someone else was thirsty. From the shed came a mournful moo. He'd forgotten to give the brown cow her water and let her out in the orchard to graze.

This needed quick thinking. If he went out to the shed, there'd be no trouble with the pig, who wasn't going anywhere. But the baby was crawling around and might tug on the churn and topple it over.

Well, Ola was more than a match for this problem. He slung the churn over his shoulder, got the bucket and went across the yard to the little stream that flowed nearby to get water for the cow.

However, as he bent down to fill the pail, the lid fell off the churn and the half-churned cream ran down over his neck.

Was he discouraged? Not he! He filled the bucket, went back to the shed, let the cow out and gave her a long drink. She thanked him very much for that.

Now it was clear to a sharp chap like Ola that he couldn't take the cow down to the orchard and leave the baby alone. But he had the answer. The cottage was roofed with turf and in the summer the turf grew grass like a little field. In two shakes he had the cow up the slope behind the cottage, and he'd bridged the gap between this and the roof with a plank. With a little urging he persuaded the cow to walk along it, and soon she was happily grazing on the roof. Down went Ola to the kitchen again.

But quick as he was, time was passing quickly too. He had to get the porridge going. So he filled the pot with water and hung it over the fire. And while he was pouring in the oats, a thought struck him.

What if the cow should slip off the roof? If that happened all his livestock would be deadstock. He didn't hang about, but took a rope and climbed swiftly on to the roof. It was a moment's work to tie one end of the rope round the cow's neck and pass the other end down the chimney.

Back in the kitchen, he took the rope end dangling down the chimney and tied it round his own leg, keeping both arms free. All was going well now. The cow was grazing on the roof, the baby was gurgling in the corner, the pig was lying – very quietly – outside the kitchen door and the porridge was in the pot. Ah, but now he needed the ladle to stir it with.

He stared across the kitchen to the row of hooks where the ladles hung. As he moved, the cow was pulled by the rope right up against the chimney. She didn't care for that and nor would you. So she pulled back just as Ola was taking down the ladle, and he was drawn across the kitchen floor towards the fireplace.

Not to be pushed around – or pulled – by a cow, Ola jerked back and set off across the room again. Up on the roof the cow braced herself and heaved in the opposite direction. To and fro they went in a mad tug of war.

But weight and four legs count. Ola's feet went from under him. The cow slipped backwards, staggered and fell off the roof,

while Ola slid faster and faster
until he shot, feet first, up the
chimney. She hung down outside
while he hung down inside.

Now, about the time that Ola had
set the porridge to boil in the pot,
Kari finished mowing Ten Acre
Meadow. The sun had climbed
right across the sky. When was Ola
coming to call her home to dinner?
There was no sign of him, so she
put the scythe over her shoulder
and set off down the valley. Soon
enough she came in sight of the
cottage.

   She stopped in amazement. She
could not believe her eyes. What
on earth was the cow doing,
waltzing around the roof like
that? And just as she asked the

question the cow *fell off* and hung at the end of her tether, swinging a few feet from the ground.

She'll choke herself, thought Kari. Running across the yard she gave one quick swipe of the scythe blade, cut the rope and the cow dropped safely down to earth.

Next Kari caught sight of the pig lying in the doorway. What was going on? As she hurried up, the pig opened one eye and looked at her – but couldn't answer the question.

Neither could the baby, who was happily playing in the middle of a pool of cream on the kitchen floor.

And neither could Ola, who was standing on his head in the porridge.

Great Aunt Bun and Trouble

Linda Greenbury

"This morning," said Great Aunt Bun, "we are going out in the car."

Great Aunt Bun was small, round and warm, just like a bun from the baker's shop.

She said, "First we shall go to the hospital. We shall go shopping afterwards. Mr Piper needs some more biscuits."

Mr Piper wagged his black tail. He liked going out with Great

Aunt Bun. Something exciting always happened. Mr Piper liked the car and he wanted some more dog biscuits. Mr Piper was very pleased.

Parker Puss was not pleased. She did not like the car. She liked to sleep with her nose under her tabby tail. Parker Puss did not like dog biscuits either.

"Cheer up, Parker Puss," said Great Aunt Bun. "We shall see Nancy's new baby brother at the hospital. You can go to sleep on the back seat of my little blue PUF car. Mr Piper will sit next to me."

Great Aunt Bun's little blue PUF car went along the road.

"Have I forgotten anything?" she asked. "My glasses are on my nose.

My shopping list is in my bag. My hat is on my head. Parker Puss and Mr Piper are in the back."

PUF's engine stopped.

"Here is the hospital," said Great Aunt Bun. "We are going to see Nancy's new baby brother. Come with me."

Mr Piper and Parker Puss and Great Aunt Bun entered the hospital. There was a desk inside

the front door. A man sat behind
the desk. He was reading a
newspaper.

"Good morning," said Great
Aunt Bun. "What is your name?"

"My name is Bill," said the man.
"Can I help you?"

"Yes, please, Bill. Where can I
find Nancy's new baby brother?"

Bill said, "We have lots of new
babies in the hospital. Nancy
who?"

"Nancy from next door," said
Great Aunt Bun.

Bill put down the newspaper. He
picked up a thick book. "This book
has the name of everyone in the
hospital." Bill shook his head.
"No, there is no one here called
Nancy Next Door."

"No! No! No!" cried Great Aunt

Bun. "Her name isn't Nancy Next
Door. Nancy *lives* next door. Let's
start again."

Great Aunt Bun began again.
"Nancy from next door came to my
house this morning. She was very
happy. She had a great big smile
on her face. I was making a
shopping list when Nancy came.
Look, Bill, I have the shopping list
in my bag."

Great Aunt Bun took the
shopping list out of her bag.

"I must find my glasses," she said.

"Never mind your glasses," said
Bill. "Give the shopping list to
me."

Bill read Great Aunt Bun's
shopping list.

"Cheese biscuits,
chocolate biscuits,

118

cherry biscuits,
cream biscuits,
crisp biscuits,
coconut biscuits,
currant biscuits,
dog biscuits."

Bill asked, "Why are you buying so many biscuits?"

"I like biscuits very, very much," said Great Aunt Bun. "I eat biscuits for every meal."

"Well then," said Bill. "You do not need a hospital. You want the supermarket."

"Supermarket!" cried Great Aunt Bun. "I want to find Nancy's new brother. Babies don't live in the supermarket."

Bill said, "Your shopping list says 'dog biscuits'. At which meal do you eat dog biscuits?"

"Grrr!" said Mr Piper.

"Shhh!" said Great Aunt Bun.

"What's that?" asked Bill.

"Nothing," said Great Aunt Bun.

Great Aunt Bun began again.

"This morning, Nancy told me about her new baby brother. He is in this hospital. I have come to see Nancy's new baby brother. Can you tell me where to go?"

Bill moved his foot under the desk.

"Grrr!" said Mr Piper.

"Shhh," said Great Aunt Bun.

"What's that?" asked Bill.

"That is Mr Piper. He and Parker Puss want to see Nancy's new baby brother, too."

Bill looked under the desk. He saw Mr Piper and Parker Puss. Bill was so angry.

"You cannot bring cats and dogs into the hospital," shouted Bill. "It will be lions and tigers next! This is not the Zoo."

"Mr Piper and Parker Puss are not Zoo animals," said Great Aunt Bun. "They are my friends."

"Animal friends are not allowed in hospitals." Bill's face was red. He was very angry. "Take them out at once."

Great Aunt Bun walked to the door. She stood there, shaking her head. "What a nasty, cross man! Zoo animals, indeed! Mr Piper and Parker Puss live in my house. We go out in my PUF car together. Zoo animals! Cross, nasty Bill!"

Little bits of Great Aunt Bun's grey hair stuck out from under her hat. Bill picked up his newspaper.

He began to read.

"Excuse me," said Great Aunt Bun.

Bill looked over the top of his newspaper.

"Oh no, not you again! What is it this time?"

"Please can I have my shopping list?" asked Great Aunt Bun.

Bill found the shopping list. He gave it to Great Aunt Bun.

"Here is your biscuit list. Now, please go away. Remove those animals. I have a lot of work to do."

Bill picked up the newspaper.

"Excuse me," said Great Aunt Bun.

"You again! I've just told you—"

"But, Bill, I have lost my glasses!"

"Your glasses?"

"Yes, my glasses," said Great Aunt Bun. "I must have my glasses to drive my PUF car. Where are my glasses?"

Bill looked for Great Aunt Bun's glasses. He looked on his desk, but the glasses were not there. He looked on the floor, but the glasses were not there.

"Have you looked in your bag?" Bill asked.

Great Aunt Bun opened her bag and looked in.

"No," said Great Aunt Bun. "My glasses are not in my bag. You must have them somewhere. You had my shopping list."

"Shopping lists are not glasses," said Bill. "Oh dear, you do get in a muddle, don't you? First you look

123

for a new baby in a supermarket. Then you bring Zoo animals into the hospital. I told you to go away and now you are back again."

But then Bill stopped. He began to laugh.

"What's so funny?" asked Great Aunt Bun.

"Your glasses," laughed Bill.

"My glasses are not funny."

"Where you have put them is funny," Bill said. "Touch your nose and tell me what you feel."

Great Aunt Bun touched her nose. She felt something round. "My glasses! They must have been there all the time."

Great Aunt Bun and Bill laughed and laughed.

"You aren't a nasty, cross man after all," said Great Aunt Bun.

"Will you let me see Nancy's new baby brother now?"

Bill looked at Mr Piper and Parker Puss.

"I will put them in my PUF car. They will not come into the hospital."

"Very well," said Bill. "You put those animals in your car. Then I shall show you where to find the new babies."

"Good," said Parker Puss. She was in Great Aunt Bun's car.

"Bad," said Mr Piper. He did not wag his tail. "I like going with Great Aunt Bun. Something exciting always happens."

"Cheer up, Mr Piper," said Parker Puss. "I am going to sleep. I shall dream about fish. You can go to sleep till Great Aunt Bun comes back. We'll go shopping soon."

"We'll go shopping when Great Aunt Bun comes back," said Mr Piper, "if she does not get in a muddle again."

Bill told Great Aunt Bun where to find the new babies. She went up lots of stairs. She asked herself, "Have I forgotten anything? My glasses are on my nose. My shopping list is in my bag. My hat is on my head. Mr Piper and Parker Puss are in the car. Good, now I shall see Nancy's new baby brother."

Great Aunt Bun stopped walking. She saw a door. It was the nursery.

Great Aunt Bun went to the nursery door. "The new babies are in there," she said. "I can hear them."

Great Aunt Bun heard sniffles and snuffles. She heard murmurs and mutters, gurgles and guggles, squeaks and squawks.

"The new babies are talking," said Great Aunt Bun. "At last I've found Nancy's new baby brother. The nursery door is open. I'll go inside."

But the door closed. A nurse stood by it.

"Good morning," said Great Aunt Bun. "What's your name?"

"What's *your* name?" asked the nurse. "And what are you doing here?"

Great Aunt Bun told the nurse.

"Have you asked Sister?" the nurse said.

"I haven't met your sister."
(Great Aunt Bun was in a muddle
again.)

"It's not my sister," said the
nurse. "Let's start again. Sister is
the head nurse. You must ask her
if you want to see one of the
babies. Please go away from the
nursery. The babies have to go to
sleep."

Great Aunt Bun looked sadly at
the door. The nurse walked away.
Great Aunt Bun was alone. She
did want to see Nancy's new baby
brother.

"Maybe," said Great Aunt Bun to
herself, ". . . just one little look."

The babies were asleep. Each
baby slept in a tiny cot. Some had
dark hair; some had fair hair. One
baby had no hair at all.

"Which one is Nancy's new baby brother?" said Great Aunt Bun. "I wish Nancy was here to tell me."

There was a blue and white dress on the wall. There was a small white cap as well. Great Aunt Bun took off her hat. She pushed her grey hair into the cap. Great Aunt Bun put the dress against her.

"It is just the right size," she said.

"Hello, Nurse," said a man. "Here are the newspapers for the ward."

The man went away. "He thinks I'm a nurse," said Great Aunt Bun. "If I'm a nurse, I must help. I'll deliver the newspapers."

Great Aunt Bun folded the newspapers. She put one at the end of each cot.

"There you are, babies," she said. "You can have a nice read when you wake up."

"Nurse, Nurse," called Sister. "Come into the ward."

Great Aunt Bun was in a bright room. Six ladies in six high beds. Each bed had a cupboard at the side. On the cupboards were fruit and cards and flowers.

"But I'm not a nurse," said Great Aunt Bun.

Sister did not hear. "Please tidy up the ward, Nurse. Everything must be tidy when I come back."

"First, I shall tidy Sister's table," said Great Aunt Bun – and she began.

She dusted the table and spilt the ink. She wiped the ink and hit the light. She picked up the light

and pushed the pencils. She put
right the pencils and touched
Sister's important papers. The
important papers fell down to the
floor.

Great Aunt Bun put them back
on the table. "I'm in a muddle
again. Let's start again," she
said.

"This time, I'll tidy the ward,"
said Great Aunt Bun – and she
began.

She put the cards in the slippers.
She put the slippers on the
cupboards. She put the fruit on
the floor. She put the
thermometers in the flower vases.
She put the flowers in the water
jugs. She put the water over
everything. Great Aunt Bun made
the ward so untidy.

Great Aunt Bun saw a lady in bed. The lady had two round things on her ears.

"Excuse me," said Great Aunt Bun, "can I see your hat?"

The lady said nothing.

"I like hats," Great Aunt Bun told the lady. "I have lots of hats at home. Please show me your hat."

In the next bed, another lady laughed. "That isn't a hat. It's a radio. The two round things are called earphones. All the hospital beds have earphones hanging on the wall. We can listen to the radio in bed."

"I've never seen a radio hat before," said Great Aunt Bun. "Can I try it on, please?"

Great Aunt Bun sat down on the bed. She put the earphones on her ears. She listened to the radio.

"Put on your radio hats, everyone," cried Great Aunt Bun. "You can hear a very funny man! Listen to the radio! Put on your radio hats!"

All the ladies in the ward put on their earphones. They listened to the radio. The funny man on the radio made them laugh.

Great Aunt Bun forgot about the muddle on Sister's desk. She forgot about the untidy ward. Nobody heard Sister coming.

Sister was angry. "What has happened here?" she said, crossly. "Cards, flowers, slippers, thermometers all over the ward. Everything is in a muddle."

Sister marched up the ward. The ladies saw Sister. They took off their earphones.

Great Aunt Bun saw Sister's feet. She took off her earphones, too.

"Where is that nurse?" cried Sister. "Did she make this muddle?"

But Great Aunt Bun had gone. She ran into the nursery when Sister was not looking. Great Aunt Bun took off the nurse's cap. She took off the nurse's dress. The babies were still asleep.

"I haven't found Nancy's baby brother yet," said Great Aunt Bun.

The baby with no hair at all opened his eyes. He smiled at Great Aunt Bun.

"You have a great big smile like Nancy from next door," Great Aunt Bun said. "You must be her baby brother. I am so glad to find you at last."

"Wake up, Mr Piper! Wake up, Parker Puss!" Great Aunt Bun said. "It's time to go shopping for the biscuits."

The little blue PUF car was ready. Mr Piper wagged his black tail. He liked going out with Great Aunt Bun. Something exciting always happened.

Parker Puss took her tabby tail away from her nose. PUF moved along the road.

It was just in time.

Sister came to the hospital door. She was looking for a very funny nurse. But she could not find her anywhere.

The Old Man
Who Sneezed

Dorothy Edwards

There was an old man who
sneezed and sneezed.
He sneezed and sneezed:
A-A-TISHOO!
AH-AH-AH-AH-
AH-AH-AH-AH-
TISH-OOO!
Just like that!
He sneezed till his eyes were wet.
He sneezed till his ears popped.
He sneezed so long and he
sneezed so loud:

He sneezed till his nose blew off
AH-AH-TISHOO.
The old man's nose blew off and
away.
It shot out of the door,
Into the street and over the road.
It just missed a bus.
It just missed a car.
It only just missed a lorry!
Across the road went that old
man's nose.
Over a pavement,
Through a front door,
Down a passage,
And right into a kitchen where a
dear old lady was eating her
breakfast, and it fell into that old
lady's cornflakes!
There it lay, the old man's nose,
all among the crispy yellow
cornflakes!

It made the old lady jump.

"Dear me, dear me," the old lady said.

"How did that nose get there?"

And she put on her glasses and looked again:

"What a *big* nose! What a *red* nose. It looks just like the nose that belongs to the old man over the road," that old lady said.

Now the old man who sneezed

was very upset when his nose blew away.

He wanted to sneeze again.

"I can't sneeze without my nose," he said.

So he began to chase it.

He ran out of the door into the street, but *he* was careful.

He let a bus go by.

He let a car go by.

He let a lorry go by.

He looked both ways and didn't try to cross the road until it was absolutely clear, even though he wanted to sneeze very badly.

He managed to AH-

He could AH-AH

But he really couldn't Tishoo!

But when the road was safe he ran over the road to the old lady's house.

But he didn't run through her front door.

He was a very polite old man.

Even though he wanted to sneeze he wouldn't go in without being asked.

Because he was polite he waited on the old lady's step.

He knocked on the old lady's door.

He rang the old lady's bell.

He rattled the old lady's letterbox.

"Have you got my nose in there?" he called.

"Come in, come in," said the dear old lady.

"I've got your nose here – it's perfectly safe.

It fell in my cornflakes and wasn't hurt a bit.

I'll put it back on for you if you like," the old lady said.

So the old man went into the old lady's kitchen and she put his nose back on for him.

"There!" she said. "That won't come off in a hurry. But how did you come to lose it?"

"I sneezed it off," the old man said.

"And I very much want to sneeze again, only I'm afraid it will blow off. I have very strong sneezes," the old man said.

"Yes my dear," said the old lady. "I see what you did – you forgot to be polite.

You were polite about not coming into my house without knocking first, but you weren't polite about sneezing.

YOU DIDN'T USE A HANDKERCHIEF.

No wonder your nose blew off."

She went to her cupboard and got him three paper ones.

"Hold those to your nose when you sneeze," she said.

"You'll be as right as rain."

So the old man held the three paper handkerchiefs to his nose.

Then he sneezed and sneezed:

"A-A-TISHOO!
AH-AH, AH-AH,
AH-AH, AH-AH,
TISHOO!"

He sneezed so loud he made the old lady jump.

He sneezed so loud that her door-bell rang by itself.

Her knocker knocked by itself.

Her letterbox rattled by itself.

All the buses in the road stopped.

The cars stopped.

The lorries stopped.

"AH-AH, AH-AH, AH-AH, AH-AH, TISH-ISH-ISH-ISH-ISHOO!"

That was the biggest sneeze of all!

But because he held the handkerchiefs close to his face the old man's nose stayed on.

Even though he sneezed again: "ATISHOO, ATISHOO."

And then again (not so loud) "ah-tishoo."

Then quieter still: "ah-tishoo."

And then so quiet only he could hear it: ". . .!"

But his nose stayed where it belonged.

And it never came off again, for he always remembered to be polite and to look for a handkerchief before he sneezed:

"AH-AH-AH-AH-TISHOO!"

Now the old lady can eat her breakfast, and the traffic can go up and down the road without anyone having to worry about that old man's nose!

Eleanora

David McKee

There was once a young
elephant called Eleanora.
Eleanora had a long trunk. Of
course all elephants have long
trunks but Eleanora's trunk was
very long. Not very, *very* long
though, not long enough to reach
the moon, nor even long enough to
go all the way round Grandpa
Elephant, but it was longer than
other elephants' trunks.

A long trunk can be an
advantage. You reach just that
little bit higher without having to

stand on a chair. This is very useful because elephants are not very safe standing on chairs and the chairs aren't very safe either.

But long trunks can also get in the way. Eleanora's trunk was always getting in the way. When she was running, sometimes the trunk would trip her up and sometimes it would trip one of the

other elephants. The elephants would shout "Oh Eleanora!" and she'd say "Sorry, I forgot."

When the elephants played Hide and Seek, Eleanora would always be found easily because she'd leave her trunk showing. "I can see you Eleanora," the seeker would laugh pointing at the trunk.

"Oh drat," Eleanora would say, "I forgot."

When the elephants walked in line, nobody wanted to be the one in front of Eleanora.

The worst thing of all was shopping. Poor Eleanora was always knocking things down in shops and saying, "Oh dear, sorry, I forgot." Some shops even had notices saying "No Eleanoras allowed inside." Even now if an elephant is clumsy and is rushing about breaking things, he gets called "An Eleanora in a china shop".

One day Eleanora was lying down having a little rest and as usual her trunk was stretched out; along came Eleanora's Aunt Sophie and tripped over it. Aunt Sophie was cross and even shouted at Eleanora which is not a nice thing to happen to you when you are right in the middle of a dream about scoring the winning goal at basketball.

"Oh! Oh! Oh! I'm sorry, Aunty," said Eleanora, "I forgot." Of course Eleanora really was sorry because having someone trip over your trunk is not exactly the loveliest treat in the world.

" 'I forgot, I forgot', that's all you ever say young lady," said Aunty Sophie. "Well, we shall just have to make you remember." Still talking to herself, she stomped off to see Eleanora's mother.

"I don't know what to do," said Eleanora's mother. "I remind her as often as I can and still she forgets. I've never known an elephant forget anything before."

"Let's go and speak to Grandpa," said Aunty Sophie. "He always knows what to do."

"Hmmm," said Grandpa Elephant after he'd heard the problem. Then he said "Hmmm" again and "Mmmm" and "Aaaah" just to show that he was thinking because he was. When his thinking was over Grandpa said,

"It's most unusual because normally elephants never forget but I once knew another elephant who used to forget things. He tied a knot in his trunk to help him remember. I suggest that Eleanora ties a knot in her trunk."

Eleanora was a very obedient young elephant so when her mother said, "Eleanora, tie a knot in your trunk!" she did so at once.

"Now that knot will help you remember," said her mother.

"Yes, Mamma, thank you, Mamma," said Eleanora and went off to play. A week passed without one problem with the trunk.

Another week passed and Eleanora was winning at Hide and Seek and running without tripping other elephants up and

she was very happy.

After a month the shops allowed her back in and there was never any problem.

Grandpa was very proud of the success of his idea. "You see," he said, "Elephants never forget, it's just that sometimes we have to help them remember."

"Oh, but I still forget all the time," said Eleanora.

"But how . . . But in that case . . . I mean . . . problems . . . you don't . . . if you see what I mean," said Grandpa.

"Oh, the knot doesn't help me remember but it does make the trunk shorter so it doesn't get in the way," laughed Eleanora.

Paul and the Hungry Tomatoes

Barbara Softly

It was summertime. Paul had taken Stumpers on holiday with him for three weeks. As a matter of fact Stumpers went everywhere with Paul. He was an elephant and Paul had had him for as long as he could remember.

For the first week of their holiday Paul and Stumpers stayed by themselves with Paul's uncle, Danny. For the second and third weeks, Paul's mother and father came down to join them in Danny's house.

Danny lived alone, except for Mrs Bunce from the nearby town, who came in to cook and clean for him, a shaggy dog called Solomon, two white doves called Dum and Dee, and two hedgehogs called Piggen and Wiggen, who came every night for their saucers of milk. Danny was very glad to have the hedgehogs because they ate up all the slugs that tried to eat his lettuces.

"This evening," said Paul, when he and Stumpers were in the garden after tea, "we could ask Danny if he will let us put out the saucers of bread and milk for the hedgehogs and wait up until they come for their supper."

Stumpers' long trunk curled with excitement.

"Stay up late after dark?" he said. "I've never seen the hedgehogs eating their supper, but I've heard them rattling their saucers when they think it's feeding time."

At that moment Danny came into the garden.

"Talking about feeding time and feeding the hedgehogs," he said, "reminds me that I've forgotten to feed the tomatoes. They will have to wait until tomorrow now, because I must finish writing some letters and then we'll go out and catch the last post. Would you like to water the lettuces and beans, Paul, while you are waiting for me?"

Danny hurried into the dining-room. Paul and Stumpers walked up the twisty path through the apple orchard to the garden shed at the foot of the red brick wall. In the shed were the garden tools, the lawn-mower and wheelbarrow, the boxes for seeds and pots for plants and the watering-cans. High up on the shelf were bottles and jars which Paul and Stumpers had been told not to touch.

"You water the beans and I'll water the lettuces," said Stumpers, as they picked up the cans and raced back to the tap outside the kitchen door. Up the path they went again to the vegetable garden, Stumpers to the row of fat little lettuces, Paul to the tall runner beans which were already climbing their poles and showing their scarlet flowers.

Against the brick wall in the sunniest part of the garden were the tomato plants which Danny had forgotten to feed.

Stumpers set down his watering-can, pushed his trunk in the top and sucked up as much water as he could to shower over the thirsty lettuces. When the watering-can was empty and Stumpers' trunk only gurgled in the bottom, Stumpers stood still and looked at the tomatoes. The plants were dark green and leafy and they had small clusters of yellow flowers on their stems. Stumpers huffed and thought.

"What are you doing?" asked Paul.

"Thinking," said Stumpers, "about tomatoes."

"If I had to wait until tomorrow before I had anything to eat, I should be very hungry," said Paul.

"So should I," said Stumpers.

"I think Danny is so busy that we might feed the tomatoes for him, don't you?" said Paul.

"Huff," breathed Stumpers. "But what do they eat?"

Paul didn't know.

"Bread and milk like the hedgehogs, peas like the doves, biscuits and bones, like Solomon?" asked Stumpers.

Paul shook his head. "They haven't any teeth, so they couldn't munch up peas or biscuits or bones. If we made up a mix – a kind of soft mix – eggs and milk and breakfast cornflakes—"

"We could pour it around them and give them something to eat. Honk!" snorted Stumpers happily down his trunk. "How many are there?"

"Ten," said Paul, counting carefully. "We'll need the big mixing-bowl for the food and a watering-can for the milk."

"Danny will be pleased," said Stumpers, as they ran back to the kitchen. "Shall we tell him?"

"No," said Paul. "We'll give him a surprise."

They found a mixing-bowl and a wooden spoon in the kitchen cupboard.

"I'll stir," said Paul. "Your trunk is so long you can reach all the shelves. I'll stir and you bring everything out here."

He sat on the step and waited while Stumpers rattled about in the larder and at last came out, his arms full of packets and cartons, his trunk carefully wrapped round three milk bottles.

"Six eggs, breakfast cornflakes, a packet of sugar and a brown loaf," said Stumpers.

"We'll give the crust to the birds," said Paul, holding the spoon in both hands to mix everything together and gripping the bowl between his knees so that it would not slide about.

"Anything else?" he asked. "It's very sticky."

There were more rattlings as Stumpers hunted in the larder.

"Salad cream," he called. "A bottle of vinegar and some orange juice."

Paul thought the orange juice would be best and it was slowly stirred into the mixture making it a soft, creamy yellow.

"Yellow mix," said Stumpers, tasting it with his trunk. "Honk!"

Then they took the tops off the three milk bottles and poured the milk into the watering-can. It was heavy and as Stumpers walked up the garden path behind Paul, the milk slopped out of the spout and made little splashes of white along the path.

The mixing-bowl was heavy, too. When Paul reached the row of tomatoes, he had to put the bowl on the ground and ladle out spoonfuls of yellow mix for each plant. Soon he had made a thick yellow circle round each stem; there were dollops of mix on most of the leaves, dollops on the flowers, dollops trickling everywhere, and a lot of dollops all over Paul. Stumpers followed behind, happily honking to himself, swinging his trunk in time to his honks, showering every tomato plant with milk.

"It's not a watering-can any longer, it's a milking-can," he said.

Then—

"Paul! Stumpers! What on earth are you two doing?"

It was Danny, carrying his letters in his hand and running up the garden as fast as he could. He did not look at all pleased.

"We thought we would feed the tomatoes tonight as a surprise for you, because we didn't want them to be hungry," said Paul, wiping his yellow-mix hands down his shorts.

Danny looked at the row of tomatoes; he looked at the yellow mixing-bowl, at the milking-watering-can, at Paul and Stumpers.

"You know who is going to be hungry now, don't you?" he said. "You are, because the shops are shut and there is no bread for your supper, no milk to drink, no cornflakes or eggs for breakfast, no sugar, no orange juice. *This* is what tomatoes are fed on."

He took down one of the sticky, black bottles from the shelf in the garden shed.

"This – mixed with water."

"Oh," said Paul.

"Ah," said Stumpers.

That night Paul and Stumpers went to bed early. They did not stay up to feed the hedgehogs, although Danny had found enough milk left in a milk-jug to give Piggen and Wiggen bread crusts and milk for their supper. Paul and Stumpers did not really have any supper. There were only biscuits and as many glasses of water as they wanted.

Stumpers curled his trunk under his arm as he settled on the end of Paul's bed.

"Feeding time for hedgehogs and feeding time for tomatoes, but no feeding time for us," he said.

"I'm glad we didn't take the doves' peas or Solomon's dog biscuits," said Paul. "The sooner we go to sleep the sooner we shall be able to go out shopping and buy our breakfast."

"Honk!" snorted Stumpers. "But it's a long time to wait."

And it was.

Red Between
the Lines

David Henry Wilson

Jeremy James and Daddy were
going on a train journey. It
should have been a car journey,
but Daddy's car had had one of its
coughing and shuddering attacks
and was now recovering in the
repair shop. Daddy had an
appointment in Castlebury, which
was fifty miles away, and so while
Mummy stayed at home to look
after Christopher and Jennifer
(she said twin babies weren't much

fun on public transport, but Jeremy James thought twin babies weren't much fun anywhere), Daddy and Jeremy James set out to catch the 10.15 train.

By the time Daddy had found his wallet, papers, briefcase and left sock, it was nearly ten o'clock, and Daddy said they would have to run to catch the train. Jeremy James didn't think he could run fast enough to catch any train, but he held on to Daddy's hand, and the two of them ran-walked and walked-ran all the way to the station.

"Three minutes to go," said Daddy, puffing like an old steam engine. "Let's hope the train'll be late."

They bought the tickets and

went panting (Daddy) and scampering (Jeremy James) up a steep slope and on to a long grey platform. This contained a few people and a lot of litter.

"Exactly 10.15!" gasped Daddy. "Train must be late. Lucky for us."

At that moment a crackly voice boomed from up in the roof: "We regret to announce that the 10.15 train to worple, worple, Castlebury, worple, worple and worple is running approximately forty minutes late."

"Forty minutes!" exclaimed Daddy. "Ugh, what a service!"

"I thought we *wanted* the train to be late," said Jeremy James.

"Well yes," said Daddy, "but not *that* late!"

Just then there was a distant

rattle that grew into a rumble that suddenly became a terrifying roar, and a train hurtled through on the other side of the track. The station and Jeremy James shook like a couple of jellies in a thunderstorm. Then the roar faded to a rumble, a rattle, and finally silence, and the station and Jeremy James stopped shivering.

Jeremy James gazed up the track with a worried expression on his face.

"What's the matter, Jeremy James?" asked Daddy.

"Well," said Jeremy James, "if the train's going *that* fast, I don't think I shall be able to get on it."

Daddy laughed. "If the train's going," he said, "you shouldn't *try* to get on it. You only get on trains that stop."

At 10.55 the 10.15 train to Castlebury stopped for Daddy and Jeremy James. It came slithering painfully into the station like a giant snake with backache, and Daddy helped Jeremy James up the high steps and into the carriage. Most of the seats were empty.

"There aren't many people," said Jeremy James.

"They've probably gone on ahead," said Daddy. "On foot."

Jeremy James sat down by a window, and Daddy sat opposite him. There was a whistle, and the train twitched, jerked, and began to slide gently out of the station.

"We're moving," said Jeremy James.

"Let us be thankful," said Daddy, "for small miracles."

In the wide frame of the window, houses and factories and back gardens gave way to fields and trees and rivers. The train diddly-dummed along, and Jeremy James leaned back and looked round. There was nothing very interesting to see – seats, tables, Daddy, the luggage rack, Daddy's briefcase on the luggage rack . . . and above Daddy's briefcase a red handle.

"Daddy, what's the red handle for?" asked Jeremy James.

Daddy followed the direction of Jeremy James's pointing finger.

"Ah, the communication cord," said Daddy. "It's so that people can stop the train in an emergency."

"You mean like wanting to wee?" asked Jeremy James.

That had happened to him once. They'd been driving along the motorway and he'd had an emergency, so Daddy had stopped at the side of the road. Then a police car had come along, and the policeman and Daddy had had a lovely conversation about emergencies.

"No," said Daddy. "If it's *that* sort of emergency, there's a lavatory at the end of the carriage."

A little while later, Daddy himself had *that* sort of emergency, and he went off, leaving Jeremy James to look out of the window. The train was going quite slowly now, past big gloomy buildings and a lot of railway lines. Perhaps they were coming into a station – one of the worples before Castlebury. Jeremy James hoped Daddy would get back before the train stopped, in case someone wanted to take his seat. But if the worst came to the worst, he could tell them that Daddy was doing an emergency.

It was indeed a station. Jeremy James stood up to get a better view. There were quite a lot of people on the platform, and Jeremy James spotted a crowd of children. The train glided by, and he waved to them. Some of them waved back, and he wished the train would stop just there, but on it went . . . and on . . . and on. And all of a sudden, they were out of

175

the station again! They hadn't
stopped at all!

Obviously something had gone
wrong. Those people were waiting
for the train, but of course they
weren't allowed to get on it unless
it stopped, and it hadn't stopped.
Perhaps the children hadn't been
waving to him but to the driver,
trying to attract his attention.
Perhaps the driver had been
looking the wrong way. Or perhaps
he was asleep. Or dead. Dead, and
slumped over the steering wheel,
while the train roared on and on
towards disaster and destruction.

There was no doubt about it, this
was an emergency. Jeremy James
leaped on to the seat, clutched the
luggage rack with one hand, put
one foot on Daddy's armrest,

heaved himself up, and was just able to reach the red handle and give it a hearty tug.

Almost at once there was a grinding screech, and it felt as if the train were trying to move backwards while everything inside it tried to move forwards. Jeremy James bounced from armrest to seat to floor, and lay there for a

moment wondering how much of himself he'd left hanging on the luggage rack. Then he picked himself up, and checked that all of him was still where it was supposed to be. He found that even his nose was still sitting comfortably in the middle of his face, and soon he was pressing it against the window to see if the children and the other passengers were coming.

Wouldn't everyone be pleased! Jeremy James had saved the outside passengers from missing their train, and the inside from disaster. When they found out what had happened, the railway people would probably give him a very big reward.

But the children and other

passengers didn't come. Daddy came, closely followed by a railway person who had not brought along a big reward. All he brought with him was a peaked cap, a bristly moustache, and a very red face. He didn't seem pleased at all. In fact he was very un-pleased. He said someone had pulled the red handle, and he wanted to know *who* had pulled the red handle, and *why* the red handle had been pulled. Jeremy James explained to him that some people were waiting for this train at the station, and the driver hadn't seen them because he was dead, and so he, Jeremy James, had pulled the red handle in order to save everybody, and would there be a reward?

The red-faced man's face went

redder, and Daddy's face went as red as the red-faced man's had been before it went redder. The people at the station, said the redder-faced man, were not waiting for *this* train, and the driver wasn't dead, and there were two passengers on this train who might end up dead after the driver had heard why the red handle had been pulled, and there would not be a reward, and grown men should learn to control their children, and there'd already been enough trouble today without . . .

The red-faced man now used a word that Daddy had once used when hammering a nail (his thumbnail) into the wall. Mummy had said that such words were forbidden, but the red-faced man obviously didn't know Mummy had forbidden such words, and after he'd said it twice Daddy went back up the aisle with him.

Jeremy James sat in the corner and looked up at the red handle near Daddy's briefcase. It reminded him of when he'd been on a bus with Mummy. Instead of a handle there'd been a bell, and when the conductor wanted the bus to stop or start he rang the bell. The thought occurred to Jeremy James that if he pulled the handle again, the train might start and the red-faced man would go away.

Jeremy James was just climbing on to Daddy's seat when Daddy came back along the aisle, looking a little sadly at his wallet.

"*Now* what are you up to?" asked Daddy.

Jeremy James explained his idea to Daddy. But Daddy didn't think it was a very good idea.

"Your ideas, Jeremy James," said Daddy, "have made a late train later, a red face redder, and poor Daddy a lot poorer. So I think the best idea, Jeremy James, is for you to stop having ideas altogether."

The train was now moving again, and so Jeremy James sat quietly in the corner and looked out of the window. It wasn't easy to stop having ideas – in fact ideas kept coming to him all the time. He had ideas about ice cream, and chicken, and sweets, and fizzy drinks. He also had an idea about saying he was sorry he'd pulled the red handle. But he didn't tell Daddy and so Daddy never knew.

The Hare and the Lazy Hunter

Lynne Reid Banks

Once there was a hunter who was so lazy, he couldn't be bothered to go out to hunt until he was practically starving.

When that happened, he would whistle up his dog.

"Don't just lie about, you lazy beast!" he would say, as the dog shambled to his side. "Get out of here and catch me some game!"

The dog, who was just about as lazy as his master, would heave a deep sigh, and walk very slowly out of the door, pausing on the way to sit down and scratch a flea.

His master would fly into a rage. "What's the use of you?" he would shout. "Get on with it, and never mind scratching your worthless hide!"

At this the dog would put on a turn of speed and run off into the countryside – run as fast as it could, until it was out of sight of the hunter's cottage. Then it would lie down and doze in the sun, hoping some idiotic creature would run so close to its mouth that he could catch it without any effort.

One day the dog was lying like that, half asleep, when a big, fat hare came jumping along the path.

The dog opened one eye and watched it, rolling its eye up and down as the hare bounded along.

"It doesn't see me!" thought the dog, although he was lying right across the path. "Perhaps it thinks I'm a log and will try to jump over me! Then I can grab its legs without even getting up!"

But when the hare had nearly

reached it, it stopped, sat down, and scratched its long ear with one long back foot. Just the way the dog did when it had a flea.

The dog forgot it was supposed to be a log and lifted its head.

"Do hares get fleas, too?" it asked interestedly.

The hare jumped in the air as if it had had a great fright.

"Goodness gracious grips!" it exclaimed. "You're a DOG! I thought you were a bit of wood."

"That's what I meant you to think," said the dog, very pleased with itself.

"You really fooled me," said the hare. "You look exactly like a log."

The dog, which was black and white, was stupid enough to believe every word the hare said.

"If you'd jumped over me," it said, "do you know what I was going to do?"

"No, what?" asked the hare, making big eyes.

"I was going to catch you by the legs and carry you home to my master, who's a hunter."

"Goodness gracious grips!" said the hare again. "How clever! How daring! And you nearly succeeded!"

"Yes! But I didn't quite," said the dog, looking crestfallen. "So now I'll have to go back to my master with nothing, and he'll be angry and beat me."

"BEAT you?" said the hare. "We can't have that! I tell you what. You pick me up in your mouth – very gently, mind – and carry me back to your master. Then he'll be very pleased, and not beat you."

The dog thought this was a brilliant idea. He jumped up, picked up the hare in its mouth – very gently – and carried it back to its master's cottage.

As it came in through the door, the lazy hunter woke from a snooze by the fire, feeling hungrier than ever. He saw the fat hare hanging from the dog's mouth.

"What! A lazy animal like you caught such a big hare! I'd never have believed it!" he exclaimed. "All right, drop it. Leave it!"

At this command, the dog let go of the hare, which promptly jumped up and began to leap about the room.

"You stupid hound!" shouted the

hunter. "You were meant to kill it! Chase it, you fool, catch it at once!"

The dog chased it, the hunter chased it, they ran all round the cottage five times, but the hare outwitted them at every turn. It made them fall over each other and bump into each other and trip each other up, until the dog was black and blue instead of black and white, and the hunter was purple in the face with rage.

"I'll get it if it's the last thing I ever do!" he vowed.

At last they cornered the hare in an upstairs room.

"Now we've got it!" panted the hunter, who had never run so fast or used so much energy in his life.

The dog and the hunter crept

towards the hare, which stood
there looking at them without a
trace of fear. At the moment when
they both made a dive for it, it gave
one last great leap in the air. It
leaped right up to the ceiling, and
they crouched, expecting to feel it
land across their backs with its
sharp claws.

But they felt nothing.

Fearfully, they both looked up.

The hare had completely disappeared.

The lazy hunter slunk downstairs, exhausted. He didn't have the strength to beat the dog. Instead he opened a tin of baked beans, but before either of them could eat any, they were asleep and snoring.

A Pet Fit For a King

Liss Norton

King Kevin wanted a pet. Not a dog or cat. Not even a budgie or a goldfish. He wanted an *unusual* pet. A pet fit for a king. He phoned the pet shop. "Please send me a special pet," he said.

"We've got a South American glitter snake, Your Majesty," the pet shop lady said. "I'm sure you'd like it."

"Please send it along to the castle," said King Kevin.

The South American glitter snake was beautiful. Its gold and silver scales glittered in the sunlight. "Perfect," King Kevin said as he took it out of the box. "This is a pet fit for a king." He stroked the snake's back and it hissed happily.

The snake was great fun. It played a game that King Kevin called hide and shriek. It hid in a cupboard and made Simmons the butler nearly jump out of his skin. It hid in the long grass and made Old Peg the gardener jump so high she landed in a tree. It hid in the kitchen and made Mrs Bakewell drop the cabbage she'd cooked for dinner. King Kevin was very glad about that. He hated cabbage.

Bedtime came. King Kevin changed into his pyjamas and cleaned his teeth. He searched for

the glitter snake but he couldn't
find it. "It must be hiding," he said
with a grin. "I expect it wants to
frighten somebody." He went into
his bedroom. He pulled back the
bedclothes. The glitter snake
sprang up with a loud hiss.
"Aaagh!" screamed King Kevin.
He fell over backwards BUMP!
and bruised his bottom.

The next morning King Kevin
took the glitter snake back to the
pet shop. "It wasn't quite right for
me," he said, "I'd like a parrot
instead."

The parrot was beautiful. It had
red, green, blue and yellow
feathers. It had bright eyes and a
curved beak. "*This* is a pet fit for a
king," King Kevin said happily.
The parrot flew on to his shoulder

and King Kevin carried it back to the castle.

The soldiers were practising their marching in the courtyard. "Quick march!" Captain Gruff commanded.

"Quick march," squawked the parrot.

King Kevin was delighted. He'd forgotten that parrots can talk.

"Right wheel," cried the Captain.

"Right wheel," echoed the parrot.

King Kevin stroked the parrot's feathery chest. "I knew you'd be a good pet," he said.

"I knew you'd be a good pet," screeched the parrot.

They watched the soldiers for a long time and the parrot learned to repeat every order he heard. At last Captain Gruff marched off to have a cup of tea. He left the soldiers standing smartly to attention.

"Quick march," the parrot squawked. The soldiers began to march. "Right wheel," shrieked the parrot. The soldiers turned right. Some of them bumped into the castle wall and had to sit down.

"About turn," screeched the parrot. "At the double." The soldiers turned round so quickly they got their swords tangled together. King Kevin laughed and laughed.

Captain Gruff heard the commotion. He ran into the courtyard. "What's going on?" he bellowed. He looked so angry that King Kevin ran away. The parrot held on tightly to his shoulder.

They hid behind the bathroom door. "The Captain will never find us here," said King Kevin.

"The Captain will never find us here," squawked the parrot.

King Kevin heard heavy footsteps clumping up the stairs. "Shhh," he hissed.

"Shhh," said the parrot.

"Don't say another word or he'll hear us," King Kevin whispered.

"Don't say another word or he'll hear us," screeched the parrot.

The footsteps stamped along the passage. They halted outside the bathroom door. "Where are you, Your Majesty?" Captain Gruff said crossly.

"Where are you, Your Majesty?" echoed the parrot.

King Kevin glared at the parrot. He didn't want a pet that gave away his hiding places. He came out of the bathroom. Captain Gruff looked furious. No more parrots for me, King Kevin thought.

The pet shop lady was surprised to see King Kevin and the parrot. "What's wrong with him, Your

Majesty?" she asked.

"He talks too much," King Kevin said.

The pet shop lady nodded. "Which pet would you like now?"

King Kevin explored the shop. There were so many different pets to choose from. He liked the scaly crocodile with the sharp white teeth. He liked the lizard that changed colour. He liked the huge hippo that yawned when he tickled its tummy. He liked the upside-down bat. He especially liked the fluffy black tarantula. But he knew they would all cause trouble at the castle.

At last he spotted a tiny brown monkey. He bent down for a closer look. The monkey sprang up. It stretched out a little paw. It held

King Kevin's finger. "I'll have this
monkey," King Kevin said. "And
I'll call him Marmaduke."

On the way back to the castle,
Marmaduke curled up in King
Kevin's arms like a baby. King
Kevin stroked the monkey's soft
fur. "No one can complain about
you," he said.

But he was wrong.

Marmaduke liked living in
the castle. He snatched the
feather duster from Polly the
chambermaid. He turned
somersaults in the courtyard and
made the soldiers laugh so much
they forgot to guard the castle. He
stole bananas from the kitchen
and left the skins where Simmons
the butler was sure to slip on
them. He even dug up one of Old

Peg's prize rose bushes.

Everyone in the castle came to see King Kevin. "That monkey has got to go, Your Majesty," they cried. "We can't do our jobs with him around."

King Kevin stroked Marmaduke's head. He really loved the little monkey and he didn't want to send him back to the pet shop. But he was the king and kings have to set a good example. "All right," King Kevin said sadly. He wiped away a tear. "I'll take him back to the pet shop in the morning."

Morning came. Sadly, King Kevin picked up the little monkey. He didn't want to take Marmaduke back to the pet shop but he knew he had to. He carried

the monkey outside. A strong wind
had sprung up during the night.
Marmaduke shivered in King
Kevin's arms. "Don't worry," King
Kevin said. "You'll be quite safe
with me. I won't let you blow
away." As he spoke there was an
extra-strong gust of wind. King
Kevin's crown flew off his head. It
whirled up into the air.

"Help!" King Kevin cried. "My
crown's blown away."

Captain Gruff and the soldiers
ran out into the courtyard. The
wind lifted the crown high above
the roofs of the castle. "The royal
crown has blown away," Captain
Gruff bellowed.

Mrs Bakewell the cook ran out
of the kitchen. She was holding a
bowl full of chocolate pudding mix

and a wooden spoon. "The royal crown has blown away," she cried.

Old Peg ran up from the garden. "The royal crown has blown away," she said.

Simmons the butler and Polly and the chambermaid peered out of an upstairs window. "The royal crown has blown away," they gasped.

Suddenly the wind dropped. The crown began to fall. It spun round and round, falling faster and faster. It landed on top of the highest tower in the castle. "Oh no!" everyone cried. "We'll never get it down from there." King Kevin knew they were right. The longest ladder in the kingdom wouldn't reach to the top of that tower.

Suddenly Marmaduke sprang out of King Kevin's arms. He ran across the courtyard and began to climb. He clambered up the castle walls. He clung to the stones. "Be careful," King Kevin cried.

The monkey reached the battlements. He clambered over. He climbed up the side of a tower. Soon he was scrambling up the roof of the highest tower in the castle. At last he reached the top. He picked up the crown and started to climb down again. "He's done it!" Polly cried.

It didn't take Marmaduke long to reach the ground. He ran across to King Kevin. He climbed up King Kevin's back and plonked the crown on his head. "The royal crown is safe!" everyone cried.

"Marmaduke is a hero. Three cheers for Marmaduke."

King Kevin stroked the little monkey's head. "Does this mean I can keep Marmaduke?" he asked hopefully.

"Keep Marmaduke? Of course you can, Your Majesty," everyone said. "He's a pet fit for a king!"

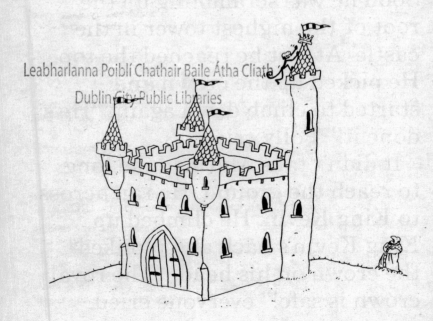

ACKNOWLEDGEMENTS

The publishers wish to thank the following for permission to reproduce copyright material:

Tony Ross: *Mrs Goat and her Seven Little Kids* by Tony Ross; first published by Anderson Press 1990 and reproduced with their permission.

Betsy Byars: "Secrets" from *Round About Six*, chosen by Kaye Webb; first published by Frances Lincoln 1992, pp. 30–7 and reproduced by permission of Betsy Byars.

Linda Greenbury: *Great Aunt Bun and Trouble* by Linda Greenbury; first published by Pitman Publishing 1972 and reproduced by permission of Linda Greenbury.

Nancy Blishen: "A Little Bit of Colour" from *A Treasury of Stories for Five Year Olds*, chosen by Edward and Nancy Blishen; first published by Kingfisher Publications plc 1989, pp. 84–9 and reproduced with their permission. Copyright © Nancy Blishen 1989.

Liss Norton: "A Pet for a King" from *A Treasury of Pet Stories*; first published by Kingfisher Publications plc 1997, pp. 48–56 and reproduced by permission of M. C. Martinez Literary Agency on behalf of the author.

David Henry Wilson: "Red Between the Lines" from *Can a Spider Learn to Fly?* by David Henry Wilson; first published by J. M. Dent 1984, pp. 1–9 and reproduced by permission of Orion Publishing Group Ltd.

Malorie Blackman: "Betsey's Birthday Surprise" from *Betsey Biggalow* by Malorie Blackman; first published by Piccadilly Press 1996, pp. 16–28 and reproduced with their permission.

Alf Prøysen: *Mrs Pepperpot Minds the Baby* by Alf Prøysen; first published by Hutchinson 1987 and reproduced by permission of Random House UK Ltd.

David McKee: "Eleanora" from *The Much Better Story Book*; first published by Westminster Children's Hospital School and Random House 1992, pp. 62–8, and reproduced by permission of Random House UK Ltd on behalf of the Westminster Children's Hospital School.

Pat Hutchins: "Three Cheers for Charlie" from *The Much Better Story Book*; first published by Westminster Children's Hospital School and Random House

ACKNOWLEDGEMENTS

1992, pp. 71–4, and reproduced by permission of Random House UK Ltd on behalf of the Westminster Children's Hospital School.

Dorothy Edwards: "The Old Man Who Sneezed" from *The Old Man Who Sneezed* by Dorothy Edwards; first published by Methuen Children's Books 1983, pp. 7–13 and reproduced by permission of Rodgers, Coleridge and White on behalf of the author. Copyright © Dorothy Edwards 1983.

Moira Miller: "Maggie McMuddle and the Chocolate Cake" from *Meet Maggie McMuddle* by Moira Miller; first published by Methuen Children's Books 1989, pp. 16–29 and reproduced by permission of Caroline Sheldon Literary Agency on behalf of the author.

Robert Leeson: "Why's the Cow on the Roof?" by Robert Leeson; first published by Walker Books Ltd 1998 and reproduced with their permission. Copyright © Robert Leeson 1998.

Lynne Reid Banks: "The Hare and the Lazy Hunter" from *The Magic Hare* by Lynne Reid Banks; first published by HarperCollins 1992, pp. 53–8 and reproduced by permission of Watson, Little Ltd on behalf of the author.

Dick King-Smith: "Philibert the First" from *Philibert the First and Other Stories* by Dick King-Smith; first published by Viking 1994, pp. 7–19 and reproduced by permission of A. P. Watt on behalf of Fox Busters Ltd.

Every effort has been made to trace the copyright holders but if any have been inadvertently overlooked the publishers will be pleased to make the necessary arrangement at the first opportunity.

Reading fun for all ages